VERMILLION
PUBLIC LIBRARY
VERMILLION, S.D.

9.93   T

W   c.1
Zimmer
Cottonwood station

DISCARDED
BY
VERMILLION PUBLIC
LIBRARY

D1058197

Vermillion Public Library
18 Church Street
Vermillion, SD 57069

DEMCO

COTTONWOOD STATION

Also by Michael Zimmer

Dust and Glory
Sundown

COTTONWOOD
STATION

Michael Zimmer

Walker and Company
New York

Copyright © 1993 by Michael Zimmer

All rights reserved. No part of this book may be reproduced or
transmitted in any form or by any means, electronic or mechanical,
including photocopying, recording, or by any information storage and
retrieval system, without permission in writing from the Publisher.

All the characters and events portrayed in this work are fictitious.

First published in the United States of America in 1993 by Walker Publishing
Company, Inc.

Published simultaneously in Canada by Thomas Allen & Son Canada, Limited,
Markham, Ontario

Library of Congress Cataloging-in-Publication Data
Zimmer, Michael, 1955–
Cottonwood Station / Michael Zimmer.
p. cm.
ISBN 0-8027-1273-8
1. Cheyenne Indians—Fiction. I. Title.
PS3576.I467C67   1993
813'.54—dc20   93-16454
CIP

Printed in the United States of America

2 4 6 8 10 9 7 5 3 1

To Vanessa,
for her strength and support

1993   aunt Coll.

Ingram

VERMILLION
PUBLIC LIBRARY
VERMILLION, S.D.

COTTONWOOD STATION

CHAPTER 1

IT WAS STILL early afternoon when Clint Dawson rode across the low Kansas ridge and spotted the grove of cottonwoods, but he knew he would travel no farther that day. He paused below the skyline, his gaze resting briefly on the trees, then lifting to sweep the shallow valley that ran to the south. Nothing stirred under the flat, cobalt sky, and after a couple of minutes he straightened and let his muscles relax. He lifted the reins of his rangy dun, and the gelding moved out with a quickened step, as if sensing they would stop at the cottonwoods for the night. A packhorse followed without lead, its head low.

Clint Dawson was a rawboned, broad-shouldered man of average height. Shaded by a wide-brimmed, sugar-loaf hat, his face was lean and angular, deeply tanned by years of exposure to the prairie winds. His sandy, sun-faded hair curled past the collar of a worn hickory shirt. Despite the loose-jointed way he sat his saddle, there was an alertness in his gray eyes, a kind of casual vigilance common to men who spent their lives wandering the fringes of the frontier.

Clint rode into the trees and dismounted. The hot August breeze stirred the leaves overhead with a dry, rattling sigh. Shifting the heavy Whitworth rifle to his left hand, he moved slowly through the grove. He gazed at the ground, reading it like a printed page. Old firepits, tipi rings, and a scattering of bones told him this was a popular camping spot for Indians, not big enough to support a village but, with a small spring near its center, a likely place for roving parties to spend a night.

1

He squatted beside the most recent fire and stirred the ashes with a half-charred stick. They broke apart like fluff, no more than a few days old. The discovery made him uneasy. He had hoped that by riding south he could avoid the Cheyenne war parties that were raising bloody hell along the Kansas-Pacific right-of-way and on the Smoky Hill Trail that linked the Missouri settlements with Denver. He wondered now if he had come too far south.

The dun nickered from the edge of the grove, and the packhorse, a little bay with a graying muzzle, pawed at the hard sod. Grinning, Clint made his way back to the horses. "Yeah, I guess it's as good a place as any to stop," he told the dun, rubbing the gelding's neck affectionately. He was still a long way from Fort Dodge, and a man had to eat and sleep, no matter how chancy the country might seem.

He let the animals drink their fill at the spring, then led them away from the spongy ground surrounding the muddy pool. He would make his camp at the edge of the trees, where the earth was firmer, the insects fewer.

Leaning his rifle against a sloping cottonwood, he lifted a stirrup over the saddle to loosen the cinch. He'd just worked a finger into the knot when a light, distant *pop* caused the dun to lift its head, ears pricked to the south. Clint paused, frowning. Picking up his rifle, he walked onto the prairie, away from the chattering leaves and the creak of saddle leather.

To the south, no more than a couple of miles away, he saw a veil of dust rising across the valley. In the clear, dry air, he could make out the blocky shape of a stagecoach pulled by a six-horse hitch and, behind it, nearly obscured by the roiling dust, what looked like thirty or forty riders. He heard a gunshot, followed by the hollow boom of a shotgun, and a distant Cheyenne war whoop.

Clint's eyes narrowed. He'd gone out of his way to avoid the main trail that ran south from Fort Hays, and half resented the coach's sudden appearance, the trouble and delay he sensed it would cause. But he couldn't turn his back on what was happening down there, and he knew Indians well enough to know they wouldn't have jumped the stage if they didn't think the odds of stopping it were in their favor.

Those folks would need some help if they were going to make it through with their scalps in place. Clint's modified Whitworth rifle, with its unique hexagon bore that could throw a slug nearly eight hundred yards, could be the help they needed. He shifted the rifle to the crook of his left arm and turned back to his horses.

Swinging onto the dun, Clint spurred toward the ridge to the west. The packhorse, snorting and kicking up its heels, followed. The stage road looked like it ran at an angle across the lower end of the valley. If it kept a relatively straight course, Clint figured he could intersect it by crossing the ridge. He might be wrong, but at the moment it looked like the best hope he had.

The dun's shoulders pumped as the gelding labored up the steepening slope, but Clint didn't pull rein until he reached the top. He found himself amid the rubble of broken cap rock, the pale slash of the Leavenworth and Pueblo Cutoff passing within three hundred yards below him. To his left he could see the stage coming toward him at a good clip. The Cheyenne were swaming around it, yipping victoriously despite the heavy fire from the coach. At least one of the harness stock—mules, Clint saw—was wounded. Its gait was choppy, erratic, and it was slowing the rest of the team.

Powder smoke blossomed from the top of the coach, where the shotgun was crouched within a shallow nest of bags, valises, and trunks, and a Cheyenne tumbled from the back of his pony. At least three others surged forward to take his place. A pistol cracked from inside the box, but the bullet plowed harmlessly into the ground.

Clint figured they stood a chance only as long as the

driver kept the mules running, but it looked like that was going to be a problem. The wounded mule's gait was roughening. Although the driver sawed at the lines, he couldn't hold the animal up. Even as Clint watched, the mule's front legs buckled; it nosed into the dirt like an anchor, dragging the rest of the team off the road. The coach followed, tipping sharply to the left as it jumped the low bank thrown up by a grader. Its left front wheel snagged a boulder, and for a moment it seemed to hang in midair. Then it toppled with a splintering crash that almost drowned out a woman's shrill scream.

Swearing softly, Clint dropped from the saddle and jerked his cross-sticks free. The overturned coach was still six hundred yards away, though being dragged closer by the panicky mules. He could see the driver clinging to the railing. The shotgun rider had been thrown free and was already climbing to his feet, surrounded by a dozen taunting Cheyenne. He must have lost his weapons in the fall, because the Indians weren't making any effort to kill him. They circled him, laughing and prodding at him with their lances, rifle muzzles, and the tips of their bows.

Clint stepped away from the dun and flopped to the ground. He set up the cross-sticks and laid the Whitworth's forestock across them. Jerking down the trigger guard to open the breech, he pulled a four-inch brass cartridge from the worn leather bag he'd set in the grass beside him and thumbed it into the chamber. Palming the breech closed, he flipped the vernier rear sight up and loosened the eyecup.

The wrecked coach had dragged the mules to a stop about five hundred yards away—well within the Whitworth's range. Quickly adjusting the rear sight, he tightened the eyecup and threw the rifle to his shoulder. His movements were swift and smooth, the result of years of experience. Cocking the jutting sidehammer, he sighted on one of the Indians surrounding the shotgun rider and squeezed the trigger.

The Whitworth roared, slamming the Indian from the back of his pony. Clint extracted the spent cartridge, thumbed a fresh one in its place, and snapped the breech closed. The sight of the fallen brave had stopped the Cheyenne. They stared at one another in confusion, then whipped their ponies around in an attempt to discover this new attacker.

Clint lined another Indian in his sights and fired again. The Cheyennes' angry howling rose to Clint's ears as the thunder of the Whitworth faded. One of the Indians spotted Clint's powder smoke and pointed toward it with his bow. He started to back his pony away, but a second warrior, riding a flashy red and white Appaloosa, stopped him. The second Indian gesticulated with a rifle, haranguing the others, then broke away from the group and rode toward the coach at a gallop. All save one followed.

Clint tried to catch the warrior on the Appaloosa in his sights, sensing that this one was a leader of some kind, but at five hundred yards the target was too small, the other Cheyenne grouped too closely around him for Clint to pick him out. Instead, Clint chose a warrior riding on the outskirts of the group, catching him behind the tiny ball of the front sight and squeezing the trigger. The 500-grain hexagon slug took the Cheyenne in the chest, flipping him neatly off the back of his pony's rump.

Several of the Indians paused, as if in confusion, but the majority of them rode on with the warrior on the Appaloosa. Still, Clint knew their confidence was beginning to unravel under the Whitworth's deadly accuracy. The warrior on the Appaloosa remained in the thick of the fighting, but many of the others were beginning to pull back. Clint let them go, concentrating on those still circling the overturned stage. He shot an Indian off a runty bay, then another off a spotted sorrel. He kept looking for the warrior on the Appaloosa, but the dust and powder smoke was too thick. He gave it up when he spotted an Indian on a buckskin trying to flank the ridge where he sat. Snugging the Whitworth to his shoulder, he squeezed the trigger, knocking the Cheyenne off his pony.

The Cheyenne attack began to break apart. Half a dozen Indians pulled away from the dusty melee and fled toward the distant line of a cottonwood-belted creek far to the south. Others followed, peeling away from the coach like flakes of rust. In less than a minute, they were all retreating.

The warrior on the Appaloosa was the last to go. He shook an old muzzle-loading trade rifle above his head, yelling angrily at those still trapped inside the coach. Then he whipped his pony after the others.

Clint thumbed a fresh cartridge into the Whitworth and slapped the breech closed. He lined his sights on the warrior's broad back, and his finger tightened on the trigger. But before he could fire something caught his attention, dragging his eyes away from the warrior. He saw the shotgun rider struggling with the Indian who had stayed behind when the others joined the fight at the coach.

The shotgun rider was scrambling away from the Indian, who followed with a tomahawk. Both men seemed to have been hurt, but it was obvious the shotgun rider was the more seriously injured of the two. Clint took a last, frustrating glance at the warrior on the Appaloosa, then swore and brought his rifle around. The Indian raised his tomahawk, Clint fired. The Whitworth's heavy slug lifted the Indian off the ground and jerked him backward like a rag doll.

CHAPTER 2

CLINT WATCHED THE Cheyenne scatter toward the distant line of trees. He counted thirty-two warriors mounted on their own ponies, but thought at least a dozen of them were riding double, either Indians who had lost their mounts, or carrying the dead and wounded.

His gaze dropped back to the wrecked coach. Gunsmoke swirled sluggishly above the overturned vehicle. The mules stood motionless and tangled in front of the stage. From the way they stood, Clint thought one or two might be wounded, but only the right leader was down.

He stood and gathered his cartridge bag, cross-sticks, and rifle. He walked over to his horse and tied the cross-sticks behind the cantle. Mounting, he settled the Whitworth across the saddlebows in front of him. He didn't trust the newfangled rifle scabbards he'd been seeing around the forts and trading posts along the Smoky Hill Trail. He liked to keep his rifle handy, where it was quick to use. Although he carried a .44 Colt in a plain black holster at his side, it was the single-shot Whitworth, reworked to accept metal cartridges, that he'd grown to trust; the Colt was a close-up weapon, and Clint figured that by the time a man needed a revolver he was already in more trouble than common sense ought to allow.

The coach's passengers were beginning to stir as Clint started down the slope toward them. A man in a buckskin jacket was moving among the mules, unhitching where he could, cutting harness when needed. He'd already led one mule aside and tied it to a vertical axle. A second man walked toward the injured shotgun rider in a curiously

hunched fashion, cradling an elbow in his free hand. The feathered shaft of an arrow jutted from the back of his shoulder.

In the coach's shadow, a woman in a flashy green dress was kneeling beside the reclining figure of a man in a dark suit. She stood when Clint appeared. He smiled grimly at the glint of sunlight rippling in her long, reddish-gold hair—hers must have been a mighty tempting scalp for the Cheyenne.

As Clint rode up, the man in the buckskin jacket stepped away from the mules and lifted a brass-framed Henry repeater in both hands. He was a bony old coot with dull white hair fanning narrow shoulders. His face was gaunt and leathery, tapering down to a pointed chin. He wore wool trousers, reinforced with leather in the crotch, a cheap calico shirt, shapeless black hat, and beaded moccasins on his feet. When Clint was still a dozen yards away, the old man lifted the muzzle of his rifle a couple of inches and said, "That's close enough, stranger."

Clint drew rein, his gaze hardening.

"Mr. Kane!" the woman said. "This man helped us. There's no need for that." She was tall, full-figured, about thirty. Despite her dusty, disheveled appearance, she seemed calm and competent.

Kane's face tightened with irritation. "I reckon I can handle this, Miz Ruby."

"Mr. Kane is our resident expert on the Wild West," Ruby said to Clint, a hint of mockery in her voice. "I'm afraid we pilgrims wouldn't know how to climb into a stagecoach without his assistance."

Kane stiffened. He swung his rifle around and said, "All right, sonny, climb off that pony, and be easy about it."

"That'll be enough!" the man with the wounded shoulder said. He had appeared soundlessly from around the coach, a slight, shuffling gnome of a man, hatless and bald, with a little round belly pushing at his checked wool

shirt. He was sweating in the sun, although Clint figured it was as much from his wound as the heat; he looked pale and drawn, his voice shaky. Yet there was no mistaking the authority in his tone. "Point that rifle somewhere else, Kane. This man saved our bacon."

"See to your mules, Booth," Kane replied, "I'll take care of this."

Booth put his hand on the butt of his holstered revolver. "By damn, you put that rifle up, Kane. There'll be Cheyenne enough to fight before the day's out, if you ain't had a bellyful of it yet."

Kane glared at the wounded man, but Booth's gaze never wavered. Finally, swearing under his breath, Kane let the rifle sag and spun away. Clint watched him stalk around the coach. "Obliged," he said easily to Booth.

"Reckon we're all kind of edgy," Booth said. He came forward, holding out his hand. "I'm Amos Booth, driver of this wrecked rig. I'd guess you're the man behind the powder smoke we saw up on that ridge yonder, a couple minutes ago."

Clint stepped down to shake the driver's hand, already liking what he saw. "Clint Dawson. Looked like you needed some help."

"Well, it was welcome, Mr. Dawson, I'll say that. I ain't so sure we could've held out without you." He looked at the Whitworth, taking in the long, heavy barrel, the polished walnut stock, and the adjustable vernier rear sight. "I've heard of such critters, but this is the first I've seen."

Clint made no effort to hand the rifle over for Booth's inspection, and the driver smiled without rancor. Turning to Ruby, Booth said, "Ma'am, if you ain't busy, I was wondering if you'd give me a hand with my young shotgun rider over there. He's cut up some, and out cold."

"You need help yourself, Mr. Booth," Ruby replied, stepping closer. She scowled at the driver's shoulder.

"You've lost a lot of blood. Come sit down by the coach and let me look at it."

"Aw, it ain't hurting, ma'am. Let's take care of Grady first."

Ruby pursed her lips. "Mr. Booth, you're in charge here, and we need you. If you don't take care of that shoulder you'll be lying beside Mr. Grady over there, and that'll leave Mr. Kane thinking he's in charge. Do you want that?"

"Why don't you do what the lady says?" Clint intervened. "I'll go help your friend." He walked past the driver before he could protest, leading the dun to the stage and tying him beside the mule already there. He let the packhorse roam, knowing it wouldn't stray far from the dun.

Clint noticed a man lying in the coach's shade. He looked to be about thirty-five or forty, pallid and loose-fleshed, like a man who'd lost too much weight too fast. He held a pistol limply in his right hand, and a wadded-up linen handkerchief in his left, spotted with blood. Consumption, Clint thought, feeling a spark of pity. Some men recover from lung sickness in the West's thin, dry air, although Clint couldn't help wondering if this one hadn't waited too long before making the trip. He nodded and spoke, and the sick man bobbed his head in reply.

"This is Mr. Wagner, of Bristol, England," Ruby told Clint, as she led Booth to the coach. "He's come out here seeking better health."

Clint nodded to Wagner, then walked toward the shotgun rider, who lay on his back close to the road. The Indian with the 'hawk lay beside him in a pool of darkening blood; stains on the grass showed Clint where the two others he'd shot had fallen, although they'd been carried off. Kneeling beside Grady, Clint studied him critically.

The young man had a dozen wounds around his chest, shoulders, and thighs—shallow rips from Cheyenne lances, each surrounded by a palm-sized patch of dried

blood. But it was the swollen knot above Grady's ear that caught Clint's attention. The kid had taken a pretty hard blow to the side of the head at some point, maybe hard enough to have caused some damage inside.

There wasn't much he could do about Grady's wounds. Most of them had already quit bleeding, although Clint knew they'd likely start again as soon as they moved him. There wasn't anything he could do about that, either. He figured Booth was right about the Cheyenne returning. They'd lost too many warriors today, and they'd want some scalps to appease the spirits of those killed. They'd be back, mad as hornets.

Clint got his hands under Grady's shoulders and lifted him. The kid groaned as his head fell back—a good sign, Clint thought. He carried him back to the coach and laid him in the shade beside Booth, who was sitting with his ankles crossed under him, leaning forward with his forehead pressed into his hands. Ruby stood above him, her face pinched with exasperation. "He refuses to remove his shirt," she told Clint angrily.

"Ain't fittin'," Booth mumbled into his wrists.

"He's about to pass out, and he won't let me look at his wound."

Clint squatted beside the driver, eyeing the arrow's shaft, cocked upward from his hunched shoulders. "Reckon you can stand it if I pull this wood out?" he asked.

"She's buried pretty deep," Booth replied.

"The arrowhead won't come with it." He glanced at Ruby, explaining, "Indians wrap their arrowheads with sinew. That softens in blood, so that when the shaft is pulled out the head stays put and keeps on cutting."

"Christ," Booth whispered.

Ruby blanched and swallowed, the tip of her tongue darting out to moisten her upper lip. Then she took a deep breath, and nodded. "I understand. So we need to get him somewhere where the arrowhead can be cut out?"

"That would be best," Clint agreed. To Booth, he said, "I'm new to this part of the country. What's our best bet out of here?"

"We were makin' a run for Cottonwood Station, maybe five miles ahead. Man named Wilson runs it. He's got a wife and a couple of kids, and at least one hired man. We'd be safe enough there. The buildings are all made outta rock. I doubt a cannonball would do more'n raise a little dust."

"Then that's where we'll try for," Clint said. He put a hand on Booth's shoulder. "Want me to try to pull that arrow out?"

"Sure, go ahead," Booth said tonelessly.

Clint looked at Ruby and saw that she understood the spot they were in. They had two men who were all but helpless, and maybe a third if Booth passed out. With the coach busted up, they had only the mules to get them to Cottonwood Station, and at least two of those were wounded; Clint could see arrows protruding from the hip of one of the wheelers, and from the neck of the off number two.

He put one hand on Booth's neck, squeezing until the driver winced in pain. With his other hand he grasped the arrow's shaft near the shoulder, jerking it upward without warning. Booth cried out as the arrow pulled free with a small, sucking sound; his eyes grew big and he swayed, reaching out with his good hand as if searching for something to grab. Ruby dropped to her knees beside him and pulled him to her shoulder.

"There, there," she cooed, as if to a child.

Booth was breathing hard against her neck, fighting unconsciousness, Clint knew. He kept his hand on the driver's neck, rubbing it gently now, as he had the dun's neck earlier, giving Booth a point of focus. After a couple of minutes Booth's breathing eased, and he began to relax.

"How are you feeling?" Clint asked.

"A mite peaked, now that you mention it," Booth whispered into Ruby's shoulder.

Ruby looked at Clint and smiled. "He'll be all right," she mouthed.

Clint nodded and stood. Booth looked as tough as an old tom turkey, and he'd likely make it okay, given a little rest. Clint didn't want to think about Grady and Wagner just yet. He walked around the coach to find Kane standing near the road, staring toward the creek where the Cheyenne had disappeared.

Kane looked around when Clint approached, hostility smoldering in his eyes.

Clint felt a moment of regret, not because he cared what Kane thought of him, but because they would need the old frontiersman's cooperation. But something was eating at Kane, and Clint suspected getting help or advice from him would be like prying rocks from a posthole.

"Got 'er all taken care of back there, sonny?" Kane jeered.

Clint ignored him. Studying the distant line of trees, he said, "What are they doing down there?"

"What makes you think I'd have any idea?" Kane flared.

"Because those are Cheyenne moccasins you're wearing, and that's an Indian-tanned jacket."

Kane's eyes shifted suspiciously. "What are you hintin' at, sonny?"

"I'm not hinting at anything. I just figured you might know the Cheyenne better than I do."

Kane's gaze darted away. "Then you figured wrong. I dont' know a damned thing about 'em."

He was lying, Clint knew, but there was nothing to be gained by pushing it. He squinted into the cloudless sky. The sun was like a huge bronzed ball, baking the land, sucking the moisture from men and animals alike. The wounded, especially, would soon be hurting. They had about six hours of daylight left, and Cottonwood Station

was no more than an hour's ride away, but there were the wounded to contend with, and more than likely the Cheyenne, before they reached the station. He said, "We're going to have to pull out pretty quick. Why don't you stay here and keep an eye peeled? I'll give you a shout when we're ready to ride."

Kane shot him a distrusting look. "I reckon not," he replied shortly. Lifting his rifle, he taunted, "You takin' over now, sonny? Figure to leave ol' Kane behind, do you?"

"You're a little jumpy, aren't you, Kane?"

"Been wanderin' these plains since before you was peein' your britches, sonny. I ain't kept my hair this long by turnin' my back on them I don't know nor trust. Uh-uh, let's you and me both go back and get things ready. Then I'll give *you* a shout when it's time to pull out."

A smile wormed its way across Clint's face. "Why, that sounds just fine, Kane. Let's go."

Medicine Wolf stalked away from the moans of the injured warriors lying scattered among the cottonwoods beside the slow trickle of the creek the People called Rattlesnake. Anger churned in him. He wanted to shriek his fury, to lift his fists toward Man Above and demand to know why He toyed with His children in this way.

They had come so close. Only a few more heartbeats and they would have overwhelmed the white man's wagon. The sweet taste of success had already touched Medicine Wolf's tongue when the shots from the ridge to the north abruptly shattered the Cheyenne attack. In helpless agony he had watched as one after another of his warriors were slammed from the backs of their ponies by the heavy slugs of the long-shooting gun.

He had tried to rally them, to make one last concentrated charge, but his braves refused to follow. This was Medicine Wolf's first raid as a war leader among the People, and by fleeing, the young men who rode with him

on this important mission had revealed their doubt in his ability to lead. That's what burned like hot coals in his stomach, but he swore to Man Above that he would not allow this shame to remain. The deaths of his fallen brothers would be avenged before Sun left this land, and he, Medicine Wolf, would carry on his lance the head of the man with the long-shooting gun.

This he vowed.

Moccasins whispered in the tall bottom grass behind him. Looks Far Man appeared at his side, his expression sober, questioning. He studied Medicine Wolf's stoic profile for several minutes before he spoke. "My brother thinks his friends have deserted him."

"Is it not true Medicine Wolf's friends ran like women when the white-eye with the long-shooting gun appeared?"

"My brother, the white-eye with the long-shooting gun did not appear," Looks Far said gently. "That is why we ran. It is not easy to fight the sting of a bee."

Medicine Wolf didn't reply to Looks Far's feeble excuse. "How many are injured?" he asked bluntly, changing the subject.

"Too many. Lone Bull, Hump, Stubs His Toe, and Spotted Owl are dead. Ugly is not among us. He stayed to kill the young white-eye who was thrown from the wagon." Looks Far held up both hands, fingers extended. "This many have felt the fire of the white-eyes' bullets. Cuts His Hair and Running Elk are hurt badly and should be taken back to the village. Yellow Knife has a broken arm."

The only outward sign of Medicine Wolf's anger was the slight flaring of his nostrils. "We cannot take Cuts His Hair and Running Elk back until we have killed the white-eyes."

"We came to kill only one white-eye," Looks Far pointed out calmly. "Does my brother forget this?"

"No, Medicine Wolf does not forget the traitor who helped lead the pony soldiers to the Washita. I do not forget the cries of the children and the old ones." His fists clenched unconsciously, the knuckles white. He would not point out that he hadn't forgotten Red Willow Woman, either, or that she had been heavy with their first child the day the soldiers ran her down on the ice-filmed banks of the Washita. Looks Far was his friend; he would know this without being told.

Medicine Wolf went on, his voice grating now with a new pain. "But neither will I forget Lone Bull and Hump, Stubs His Toe and Spotted Owl and Ugly. These men were Medicine Wolf's brothers, and I will see that the white-eyes pay for their deaths. All of them."

Looks Far nodded; he understood. "I will tell the others."

"The wounded must look after themselves. We will return for them when the white-eyes are dead."

"I will tell them," Looks Far replied softly.

CHAPTER 3

THEY RIGGED A stretcher out of the black canvas that had covered the boot and the iron railing from the top of the coach, slinging it between the two wheelers, front to rear. Sweat tracked Clint's face by the time they finished, darkening the material of his shirt beneath his arms and along his spine. He made a last circle around the two mules, checking the brass-buckled tugs and the crude, hurried stitching of the canvas, then stepped back to regard their handiwork.

"It'll do," he said.

"Travois woulda worked better," Kane drawled cynically. He'd fished a plug of tobacco from his shirt pocket while Clint checked the tugs, and pared off about an inch. With the tobacco snug in his cheek, he added, "We coulda been on the road by now."

Clint swallowed down his irritation. The stretcher had been harder to rig, but it would be quicker once they got started. Kane knew that, but he still tried to goad Clint into an argument. Still, the old frontiersman was right in one regard, they'd lost more than a half hour constructing the stretcher, time they could ill afford. "Let's get the kid loaded," Clint said abruptly.

Amos Booth sat beside Grady, his hand resting lightly on the shotgun's shoulder. He looked up as Clint approached. "Ready?" he asked.

"Just about." Clint hunkered down beside the youth. So far as he knew, except for that one brief moan when Clint lifted Grady's shoulders to drag him back to the coach, he hadn't shown any signs of coming around. But his chest

17

was rising and falling evenly, and he seemed to be resting comfortably. That was something, Clint told himself.

Booth seemed stronger, too. Although pale yet, he didn't look quite so green around the gills, and his voice had lost its shakiness.

"Are you going to be able to ride?"

"I reckon I can hang on"—Booth grimaced slightly—"though I'd damn near rather hoof it than ride one of those hammerheads bareback."

Clint grinned. "It won't be long."

"That depends on the toughness of a man's butt, I reckon." Booth looked at Wagner and chuckled. "At least it ain't no English butt, huh, Mr. Wagner?"

Lips twitching with a smile, Wagner replied dryly, "Truthfully, I've never considered the difference between an English posterior and that of the American counterpart. Perhaps you could enlighten me someday."

Booth guffawed, cocking his brow toward Clint. "I'm growing to like this Englishman, Mr. Dawson."

"Why don't you call me Clint, so I can call you Amos." He shifted around to face Wagner. "You too, Mr. Wagner."

"I'd be delighted, but only if you return the kindness. My Christian name is Jerome."

They shook hands, and Clint said, "You're looking a little stronger."

"The rest has done me a world of good. I'm afraid coach travel excites the condition, but I'm feeling wonderful now."

"Are you feeling up to some hard riding?"

"Most assuredly."

"Come on, Jerome," Booth said, struggling to his feet. "Let's you and me share a mule so we can hang onto one another. If you ain't ever rode a Missouri mule, you're in for a treat."

"Then I shall view it as such," Wagner replied gamely, rising, "and consider any discrepancy as mere oversight."

"Whew-haw," Booth whispered when Wagner had moved out of earshot. "I don't understand more'n about half of what that little English toad says, but he's got grit, I'll say that for him."

"He'll need it before we're through. Stay close to him, Amos. I expect he feels worse than he lets on, and he might need some help."

Ruby led the wheelers close, and Clint and Kane lifted Grady onto the stretcher. There was a moment of expectant silence while the wheelers pranced nervously under this new load, carried so foreignly, but when they settled down, the stretcher remained intact, the stitched canvas taut as a drumhead. Clint strapped Grady to the stretcher, using pieces of leather cut from the harness.

Booth and Wagner were already mounted double on the left leader. Ruby fetched the near number two and eyed the huge brute uncertainly. Clint went to the mule and moved the tugs out to their last hole. "They're a little high, but you can use them like stirrups," he told her.

"Like an English saddle," Wagner said, beaming at the others. "By jove, this is sport, isn't it?"

"I'm afraid I'm not used to riding astride," Ruby confessed.

"Don't you worry none about that, ma'am," Booth said. "These is special circumstances."

Clint met her eyes and felt something solid and unfamiliar buck inside him. He forced the feeling to a standstill, the way he would a rank horse. But she saw the look, recognized it, and her cool eyes warmed.

Kane's guffaw broke the moment. Turning deliberately to Clint's packhorse, he said, "I never did care for a mule."

"You don't have to ride a mule," Clint replied impassively. "You can always walk." He bent and cupped his hands. Ruby stepped into them and he boosted her onto the mule, helping her slide her feet into the tugs. He was surprised by their smallness and tried not to notice her narrow ankles or the sleek shape of her calves encased in dark silk stockings. Handing her the reins, he said, "Can you handle these?"

Ruby nodded. "I'll be fine."

Clint mounted the dun and took the lead rope of the front wheeler. Grumbling under his breath, Kane flopped aboard the last mule. Clint ran his gaze over the unlikely crew. Booth was carrying Grady's double-barreled shotgun, and both he and Wagner were armed with handguns. Kane had his repeating rifle butted to his thigh, with a cartridge belt of twinkling brass cartridges strapped around his stomach, above a gunbelt holding an outdated Colt Baby Dragoon. Clint had his Colt and the Whitworth. Ruby carried a single-shot cap-and-ball pistol Clint had found next to the tomahawk-wielding Indian, with its bullet pouch and powder horn draped over her shoulder. Handing the wheeler's lead rope to Booth, Clint rode back to the stretcher. Someone had removed Grady's gunbelt and tucked it by his side. Leaning from the saddle, Clint picked it up and brought it back to Ruby. "Do you know how to use one of these?"

"Yes."

"Then you'd better strap it on. It'll do you more good than that old horse pistol."

He rode back to take the lead rope from Booth while Ruby strapped the gunbelt around her waist. As they rode away from the coach, Clint studied the line of trees to the south. Nothing stirred, not even a hint of dust, but he had no doubt that they were being watched. Clint called Booth to his side.

"What's that creek down there?"

"Injuns call it Rattlesnake, but it's Cottonwood on any map I've seen."

"How often does the road cross it before reaching the station?"

"Twice. Three times, if you count the crossing right at

the station, but we'll be under the protection of those inside when we get there."

Maybe, Clint thought, if the Cheyenne hadn't already hit the station. He said, "Let's swing wide and stay away from the creek as much as possible."

Booth dubiously scanned the rolling dun-colored hills that climbed slowly to the west and north. "I dunno. Seems like we ought to stay with the road. It's straightest and quickest. I ain't hankerin' to wander too far away from my landmarks."

"We'd stand a better chance if we kept to open country," Clint explained. "My rifle's accurate out to eight hundred yards, and I can load and fire ten, twelve times in a minute, if I have to. That's a lot of lead for a war party to ride through."

Booth scratched thoughtfully at his jaw. "These people are my responsibility . . ."

"That's right," Clint replied impatiently.

"Now, don't get your hackles up. I ain't necessarily arguin', I just don't want to get lost out there."

We'll be less likely to be ambushed if we shy clear of the creek," Clint pointed out.

"Such as we were at the last crossing," Wagner commented from behind Booth.

Booth sighed. "I ain't forgettin' that, damnit. Okay, Clint, we'll try it your way. Lead out, and we'll follow."

Clint rode north, skirting the ridge where he had made his stand against the Cheyenne. He wanted to swing past the spring where, only a short time before, he had hoped to camp for the night. They'd water the stock there, and slake their own thirst, before pushing on.

He wanted to make a loop to the north, maybe trick the Cheyenne into thinking they were trying for Fort Hays or Fort Larned, before turning back to the station. According to Booth, they were only five miles from there as the crow flies; detouring away from the creek wouldn't more than

VERMILLION
PUBLIC LIBRARY
VERMILLION, S.D.

double that. Give them two hours, Clint thought, glancing back to the line of trees where the Cheyenne had disappeared—that much, and they'd be riding into Cottonwood Station with daylight to spare.

It had all changed, Clint thought as he led the others into the trees surrounding the spring. In the space of about an hour the quiet tranquillity of the little grove had disappeared so completely he had to wonder if it ever existed at all.

Wagner slid from the back of Booth's mule and fell against a sapling. His breath wheezed thinly in the still air beneath the trees, and his skinny legs trembled. His face looked pale, his eyes feverish. The handkerchief he clutched in his right hand was spotted with fresh blood.

Dismounting, Booth led his mule to Clint's side. "He's gettin' worse," the driver said in a worried voice. "At this rate he won't make it to Cottonwood."

"He'll have to do the best he can," Clint replied.

Booth nodded soberly. "That I'd reckoned," he said without enthusiasm. Taking the lead rope from Clint's hand, he led the mules carrying Grady's stretcher away.

The dun had been watered only a couple of hours before and hadn't been run the way the coach mules had. Clint held the big gelding back so that the more parched stock could be watered first. He walked to the edge of the trees and looked south. The stage was hidden by the curve of the ridge where he'd opened fire on the Cheyenne, and the line of trees flanking Cottonwood Creek had disappeared in the sun-hammered distance. Heat shimmered off the valley's floor, distorting the horizon and creating a blue, lakelike mirage where only a sea of curly buffalo grass waved. There was no sign of the Cheyenne.

"Such a desolate country."

Clint turned. Ruby stood a few feet away. Grady's Colt hung low on her right hip. She had made an attempt at straightening her dress and repinning her hair, but had missed a smudge of dirt on her chin.

She came closer, smiling warmly. "I haven't thanked you for what you did. You could've just ridden on and pretended you didn't see us."

"I thought about it."

"Hmm, I doubt that." She held out a gloved hand. "I'm Ruby Jennings, of Arrow Rock, Missouri."

"Glad to meet you, Miss Jennings."

"Missus, but widowed, and you can call me Ruby."

Clint felt an unexpected surge of warmth move through him. He couldn't remember the last time he had felt this way toward a woman. Maybe before the war, when he had been young and naive. There had been a girl—Sally, her name had been—who lived down the road from his family's small farm. . . .

Ruby's eyes were twinkling. "You're thinking of something. If you tell me I remind you of your mother, I'll shoot you."

Clint laughed and shook his head. "No, it wasn't my mother." He looked away.

Ruby shrugged again, changing the subject. "You think they'll come back, too, don't you?"

"More than likely. I figure they're just waiting to see which way we jump."

"Kane says we should have made a run for it, that we could have been halfway to Cottonwood Station by now."

Clint's eyes narrowed. So it was coming to that already, he thought bitterly. Well, Kane was a problem he could deal with later. Right now he had more pressing problems.

Misreading his silence, Ruby said, "Don't let Kane get to you, Clint. Something's been eating at him ever since we left Leavenworth."

"Kane isn't the problem." He glanced behind him, into the trees. Wagner was sitting with his back against the sapling, his head tipped back and his eyes shut. Booth was checking on Grady, but his movements were slow, almost clumsy; he already looked about played out, and they hadn't come two miles yet. And on top of that, the number-two mule, the one with the neck wound, was beginning to weaken. Kane had plucked the arrows from both wounded mules, but the sharp arrowheads had remained, cutting deeper with every step. Clint had considered switching one of the mules with his packhorse, but the little bay was only green broke, and now wasn't the time to see how much it would tolerate. They would just have to press on as best they could and worry about what came of it when it did.

Booth returned from the spring. He had lost his hat somewhere during his run with the Cheyenne, and replaced it with a red bandanna that he'd wrapped around his forehead, pulling a corner back and tucking it under the knot at the base of his skull to protect his bald pate from the sun. He tugged self-consciously at the bandanna as he came up, clearing his throat loudly.

Smiling, Ruby stepped aside. "It's all right, Mr. Booth. Mr. Dawson and I were just chatting."

"Well, I hate to interrupt, but I reckon we ought to roll." He fixed Clint with a steady look. "What did you have in mind?"

Clint nodded toward a low saddle to the north of them, the same saddle he'd crossed coming into the valley. "We'll ride over that like we've got all day, then swing back and make a run for the station. Things work out, the Cheyenne will think we're making a break for one of the forts to the north or east. If they ride that way to head us off, we should make it into Cottonwood Station without trouble."

Booth ducked his head, toeing a half-exposed root. "Kane says we ain't gonna fool 'em that way," the driver said. "He says they'll be waiting for us between here and Cottonwood. I, ah, I ain't partial to Kane. I reckon you know that. But judgin' by his moccasins and all, I figure he savvies Injuns some. I got to consider what he says. It's his neck, too."

"What's he saying?" Clint asked shortly.

"Says we ought to hole up here till dark, then try to slip out quietlike."

Clint's head rocked back in surprise. "Christ, Amos!"

"Now, I ain't sayin' that's what we're gonna do, but it's something to think about, considerin' Grady and Wagner."

His voice taut, Clint said, "I bought some time with my rifle, but not much. We've got to take advantage of what we have before the Cheyenne get themselves fired up again. Right now they're confused, maybe arguing among themselves about how they should make their next move, but once they decide, they'll be down on us like a Texas twister."

"You said yourself you could hold 'em off with that rifle of yours," Booth argued stiffly.

"For a while, but not forever. And not after dark."

"Injuns don't like to fight after dark," Booth replied stubbornly.

Clint's frustration soared. Only a moment ago he had dismissed Kane's dissent as an irritant, no more menacing than the buzzing of a green-head on a summer's afternoon. Now, abruptly, it had become as dangerous and life-threatening as the Cheyenne. Their only chance for survival lay in reaching Cottonwood Station before the Cheyenne regrouped. Kane had to know that, yet he was deliberately sabotaging their efforts. It didn't make sense to Clint.

Patiently, trying to keep his voice calm, Clint said, "If they get around us, surround us here in these trees, we're stopped, Amos. I can't shoot over ridges or down winding arroyos. We've got to beat them to Cottonwood Station. If we stay here, we'll all be dead before the sun comes up in the morning."

Booth's shoulders sagged. "All right, goddamnit," he growled. "We'll do it your way."

From behind them, Kane laughed derisively. Clint and Booth swung around to face the old frontiersman. Pointing with his chin, Indian-style, Kane indicated the top of the ridge where Clint had made his stand against the Cheyenne. Following his gaze, Clint felt his heart sink a little. He knew before he looked, before he even heard Ruby's sharp intake of breath, what he would see.

A single Cheyenne warrior sat his pony atop the ridge, etched sharply against the deep, clear-blue sky, as motionless as stone.

"You wasted too much time worrying over the sick and wounded, sonny," Kane announced sardonically. "Now it's too late."

CHAPTER 4

BAD LUCK HAD dogged them all summer. First there had been that little fracas with the cherub-faced army lieutenant in Leavenworth. Nothing serious, but wanting to keep a low profile, they'd slipped out of town in the middle of the night. Three weeks later they'd had that misunderstanding over cards in a Fort Scott saloon. Some blood had been spilled that time, and once again they'd pulled up stakes in the middle of the night, keeping one step ahead of the law.

Then there'd been the bank job in Iola . . .

Rusty Cantrell swung down from the stocky pinto he'd bought back at Fort Scott and put both hands against the small of his back, pushing at his spine. He let his gaze drift surreptitiously over the four men who had dismounted with him. A couple of them moved aimlessly back and forth beside their horses; the other two just stood quietly, staring into the distance as if drugged. Taking in their gaunt, stubbled faces and their trail-worn clothing gave Rusty a pretty fair picture of what he probably looked like. Weariness, bone-deep and mind-numbing, gripped them all.

Licking at his chapped lips, Rusty looked away. He wondered how long it would be before they turned on him, blaming him for everything that had gone wrong. Soon now, he thought.

Iola had been a good job gone bad, all right. It had looked easy when he scouted it—a couple of tellers, the president in his side office, whatever customers wandered in. Hit it early, just after opening, and he figured they'd be in and out of town in under fifteen minutes. With luck, they wouldn't even fire a shot.

But what was it they said about Lady Luck being fickle as a whore? Only a year ago he had been living in a three-room, second-story Chicago apartment, drinking good whiskey with his meals and enjoying the finest whores in the best houses. It hadn't fazed him to blow forty or fifty dollars a night at the gaming tables, either—he could afford it.

Only a year ago, and look at him now. No better than any flat-poked cowboy riding the grub line. And to add insult to injury, he'd been recognized in Iola. No doubt the man who'd recognized him had been the one who'd tipped the law to them. Gambling left a passel of ill-tempered losers along a man's backtrail, Rusty reasoned, and this one—he couldn't even remember the name any-more—had lost a sizable chunk of his wages back in Fort Scott. Rusty hadn't figured out yet how the gambler knew they'd planned to rob the bank in Iola. Maybe, deep into a bottle, one of his men had talked too much and let the information slip. Or maybe the Cantrell gang had more of a reputation than he'd realized. It was something to con-sider, Rusty decided.

"You should have killed him," Clyde Cooper had told Rusty flatly while they shifted their saddles to fresh mounts at the first relay.

"That's the trouble with you, Rusty," Shorty Phelps said in that brittle voice of his. "You'd be a good man if you didn't worry so much about hurting other folks."

Worrying about hurting others had never been a prob-lem for Shorty. He was the coolest killer Rusty had ever met, and he'd seen his share during the war. Shorty was a runt of a man who spent a good part of his life making up with his Colts for what the Lord had neglected him in inches. He was quick as a copperhead, and just about as mean. Even being friendly with Shorty, which was still a far stretch from being friends with him, Rusty was afraid of him. He figured a man would have to be half crazy not to be.

He didn't feel that way around the others—Clyde and Abe Aaron and Frank Cassidy. Of course, he'd known them a lot longer. Clyde Cooper, he'd met before the war. Clyde was a tall, barrel-chested man, always heavy but never quite fat. He had a round, beefy face and tiny eyes that became nearly lost in the bulge of cheeks and brows when he was angry, which wasn't often. Clyde was a pretty easygoing man, although he was sometimes rough with his women.

Abe was dark-haired and coarse-featured, a quiet, brooding man with large, fight-scarred hands. His eyes were black and opaque, his nose lumpy from past breaks. Abe had always been fond of the bottle, but lately that fondness had slipped into something darker and more sinister—sadder too, when you thought about it. Abe rarely visited the whores anymore when they rode into town flush from some Midwestern bank job, but he could suck money out of a bottle faster than any man Rusty knew.

Frank was the odd one of the bunch. He was a heavy, slope-shouldered man in his late twenties, with blue eyes, curly brown hair, and a quick, rippling laugh. He should have been a likable man, but there was something shady about him, something not quite sincere in his smile, that put most men off. Frank would spend his last dollar buying you a drink, then cut away at you with subtle insinuations until you bought him one in return. It was enough to make you want to slap him across the face, Rusty often thought, but of course with a man like Frank, you'd want to have your pistol drawn before you started your swing.

It was a strange crew to be saddled with, but a good one in its way. They were a little touchy sometimes, but that was all right, too. It kept them all sharper, quicker.

Clyde had been staring at his saddle for several minutes. Now he stirred, sniffed, and spat. "All I can say is, we'd better find us some water and grub pretty soon," he croaked, glaring at Rusty.

Rusty stepped away from the pinto and pushed his hat off the back of his head to hang by its drawstring. Dappled sunlight glinted in the heavy copper curls that fell to his shoulders. He spread his legs for balance, keeping his right hand close to his Colt. He was glad it was Clyde who'd voiced his discontent first. He could handle Clyde a hell of a lot easier than he could Shorty or Abe. "Or what, Clyde?" he asked softly.

Clyde said, "Shit," and looked away. "Damnit, Rusty, I'm hungry. I ain't had a solid bite in three days."

"Well, I'll tell you what," Rusty said in a lightly mocking tone. "I ain't too worried about you right now. It's the horses I've been thinking about. We've been pushing them awful hard the last few days, and they're about played out. If we don't switch before long, we're going to end up hoofing it out of here."

"Maybe we should've gone south," Frank said. "To the Nations."

"We've been to the Nations, Frank. It's worse than being hanged."

"Let's just go on to Colorado, like we decided," Abe said. "I was getting tired of looking at the same country all the time, anyway."

"Well, this sure as hell is something different to look at," Shorty acknowledged.

It was that, Rusty thought. He had never been west of Lawrence until fleeing the Iola job, had never really been able to comprehend the emptiness of this raw, harsh country, even though he'd heard tales about it all his life. Everywhere a man looked there was nothing but the monotonous roll of prairie, toasted a light, tannish brown by the ever-blazing sun. Twice today they'd seen small herds of buffalo in the distance, and there were always a few trees growing along the creeks, although even these were becoming more scarce as they forged deeper into the plains. Mostly, there was nothing except the land and the sky. Rusty found something vaguely intimidating in that. He had never worried too much about posses or the law, but this was different. A country like this could swallow them all.

"It might be different, but it ain't much," Frank amended. He turned a baleful eye toward Rusty, adding, "What if it's like this in Colorado? What if there ain't no green mountains where it's cool all summer? Hell, if it's like this, I'd just as soon go back to Missouri."

"There's nothing for you in Missouri except the gallows, Frank."

"They've got to catch me first, and they've been trying to do that for a good long time."

"I ain't going back," Rusty said evenly. "If anyone here wants to, I ain't twisting their arm to stay."

"Aw, hell, no one's trying to duck out," Clyde answered. "But we've gotta get something to eat. Goddamnit, Rusty, let's go shoot a buffalo."

"I'm not a hunter, and neither are you." He nodded across the narrow flat separating them from the Leavenworth and Pueblo Cutoff, winding along the base of hills that fingered up from the creek where they'd stopped. "Next stage station we come to, we'll ride in and get us some grub and fresh horses. It ain't likely they've heard about Iola yet."

Clyde and Frank shifted uneasily at mention of the town. Rusty couldn't fault them. It was at Iola that all their bad luck had come to a head.

It had been just after eight o'clock in the morning when they rode into town, but it was already hot and muggy. The clopping of their horses' hooves on the hard-packed dirt street echoed hollowly between the buildings as they entered the business section. There wasn't much traffic, and in looking back, that should have been a warning. But they'd never run into trouble *before* pulling a job, and it just never occurred to them that the law might be onto them. Rusty remembered passing a man in a rattling Studebaker wagon about a block east of the bank. He'd looked like a farmer, but he carried a shotgun across his lap and had a revolver cushioned on his coat on the seat beside him—another warning overlooked, Rusty realized now.

The drew rein in front of the Iola National and looked up and down the street. Except for an eight-yoke team of oxen pulled hastily to one side and a few chickens pecking in the dust in front of a feed store, there wasn't any livestock in sight, not even a dog. A couple of men in ankle-length dusters—warning number three, considering the heat and humidity—stood in front of the barbershop, and a shopkeeper nervously swept the boardwalk in front of his business. They didn't see a woman or child anywhere.

"Quiet town," Shorty observed mildly.

"That's the way I like 'em," Frank replied.

They left Clyde with the horses in front of the bank. Frank rode down the street and halted in front of the hardware store. Rusty, Abe, and Shorty went inside, pulling their masks over their faces as they entered.

Rusty took one look at the granite-jawed man standing inside the teller's cage and knew immediately that something was wrong. These weren't the pasty-faced tellers who'd stood there the week before when he'd wandered in to cash a money order. Rusty froze, and for what seemed like an age but couldn't have been more than a second or two, no one moved.

It was stifling inside the closed confines of the bank; the silence was charged with tension. Shorty sensed it too, and swallowed audibly, but Abe's senses had dulled since he'd taken to the bottle. Stepping to the right, as he always did, he whipped out his revolvers and announced in a booming voice: "All right, this is a holdup! Nobody move!"

Rusty swore as he dropped the canvas sack he'd hoped to fill with money. He pulled his right-hand revolver and snapped a shot at the flint-eyed man behind the teller's window just as he leveled a sawed-off shotgun above the counter.

"Get outta here!" Rusty bellowed, but his words were lost in the roar of gunfire. Powder smoke clouded the room. Lead screamed past his ears and smacked into the woodwork. In the first fusillade a bullet nicked his hat brim, another scuffed the leather of his gunbelt, and a third shattered the cuff button on his right shirtsleeve. Ducking low with a Colt in each hand, he sprinted for the door, firing recklessly into the billowing gun smoke.

Shorty and Abe were already outside, trying to swing onto their dancing mounts while returning fire. Rusty had chosen a flea-bitten gray with a trace of thoroughbred discernible in its long, sleek limbs as his getaway horse. Clyde was holding the gray's reins and his own lunging mount with one hand, and firing down the street with his other. Rusty yanked the gray's reins from Clyde's hand and vaulted into the saddle. It was then, mounted and fighting the gray, that they heard Rusty's name being called out by the poker player from Fort Scott. Rusty spun and saw the man standing at the mouth of an alley, reloading an old Civil War Springfield.

"That sonofabitch!" Clyde shouted, snapping a shot at the man.

"Forget him!" Rusty yelled. The damage had already been done, and it was too hot—lead hot—to think about revenge. Rifle fire spit at them from a dozen different directions. Bullets drilled holes in the street around the hooves of their plunging, fear-crazed mounts. The gray wanted to bolt, and Rusty let him.

They pounded east, back the way they had come. Shorty rode beside him, a pistol in each hand. Frank brought up the rear, and his shotgun thundered as he raced past the bank.

The sound of gunfire momentarily quieted as they left the bank behind, then Rusty spotted the Studebaker they'd passed coming into town. It was slanted into the street about a block away, the horses unhitched and led to safety. Its bed bristled with rifle barrels. Swearing, Rusty sawed back on the reins, pulling the gray to a lunging, head-tossing stop. An alley opened on his right, and he turned into it. The others raced after him, riding low in their saddles while lead sang around their ears and splattered off the red brick wall of a doctor's office.

The alley spilled into another street and they turned back to the left. Rusty's eyes were glued to the corner where the men who had been hidden inside the Studebaker would appear if they came after them.

There was a flurry of movement at the corner just as they pulled even with it, and Rusty lifted his Colt but held his fire. It was only a couple of kids, twelve years old or so, who had run around the corner to catch a glimpse of the fleeing outlaws. In a split second, the pistols of Frank, Abe, and Clyde exploded in Rusty's ears . . .

Something wrenched sharply inside him, and he jerked the pinto's head out of the tall bottom grass. "Let's go," he said quietly, but with an edge. He gathered the reins above the pinto's neck. "Time's wasting."

Sensing his changed mood, no one argued. They rode out of the trees and into the sunlight, angling across the flats toward the stage road.

"Quiet country," Shorty observed mildly.

"That's the way I like it," Frank replied.

CHAPTER 5

THEY WERE A sober lot as they rode out of the little grove of cottonwoods. Clint led, keeping the dun to a fast walk. He pulled the stretcher mules behind him. Ruby rode to one side, keeping an eye on Grady. Amos Booth, with Wagner seated behind him, and Kane brought up the rear, riding side by side.

Clint kept his eyes on the lone Cheyenne warrior who sat his chunky, short-coupled mustang like a statue, with only the slight fluttering of a single eagle feather tied near the head of his lance to add a sense of reality to the scene.

Near the top of the saddle, Clint glanced over his shoulder, trying to gauge how well the others were holding up. Ruby looked strangely numbed, as if the reappearance of the Cheyenne was almost more than she could handle. But when she saw Clint look at her, her lips thinned into a tight smile. She would hold up, Clint decided.

Amos Booth would hold up, too, if his wound didn't worsen. A slowly spreading patch of blood had appeared at the driver's shoulder since leaving the wrecked coach, but it hadn't grown alarmingly.

Wagner rode silently behind Booth, swaying slightly with the motion of the mule. Determination and pain were etched equally across the Englishman's pallid face. His cough was a low, steady accompaniment to the creak of leather and the hollow thudding of hooves.

Of them all, only Kane showed any sign of breaking. His voice had risen to a shrill, accusing whine when they'd discovered the Cheyenne watching them from the top of the ridge, and his gaze had darted desperately between

Clint and Booth. "We're stuck here now, Dawson," he'd charged at last. "You and your damn high-and-mighty ways have sucked us into this trap."

Ruby gasped. "Why, that isn't so, Mr. Kane. You yourself just said we should stay where we're at."

Kane lifted his rifle muzzle toward the stretcher, then let it swing to Wagner. "What we shoulda done was leave them two back on the road. We coulda been to Cottonwood by now if we had."

Booth stiffened, his eyes flashing anger. But he kept his voice level as he replied, "We won't leave the wounded, Kane, but you're free to walk out of here if you want."

Kane's gaze shifted suspiciously between them. "Walk?"

Booth's smile was taut. "You didn't think I was going to give you an L&P mule, did you?"

"Why you sonofa—" Kane started to bring the Henry's muzzle toward Booth. Booth and Wagner, who had awakened and struggled to his feet at the level of panic in Kane's voice, put their hands on their revolvers. Clint's grip tightened on the Whitworth. He was close enough to use it as a club if he had to. But Kane stopped before bringing the rifle all the way around. Glowering, he turned back to Clint. "So that's the way it's going to be, huh? Well, I'll tell you something, sonny. Ol' Kane, he don't buffalo too damn easy. You keep that in mind."

Only after Kane had stalked away from the group did the others relax. Clint still remembered Wagner's words as Kane moved out of earshot: "Nearly as dangerous as your aborigines, that one, eh?"

Clint's gaze moved to the old frontiersman now. He felt uneasy having Kane at his back, and was counting on Booth to keep an eye on him.

They paused at the top of the saddle. Before them the land stretched away like a tawny, motionless sea. Buffalo grazed in small bunches in the distance, like cloud shadows draped over the rolling hills. Behind them, and from this height, they could see above the shimmering heat waves to the broken line of trees that bordered Cottonwood Creek. The land between them and the Leavenworth and Pueblo Cutoff was empty, the ridge startlingly bare.

"He's gone," Ruby said in surprise.

"Gone for help is where he's gone," Kane grumbled.

"Ain't no more'n we expected," Booth added. He looked at Clint. "What about it? Do you still want to make a try for the station?"

"There's no other choice," Clint said. He knew Booth was thinking about Fort Hays to the north and Fort Larned to the east. They were taking a chance that the stage station hadn't already been hit by the Cheyenne, and that there would be help there when they arrived. It was enough to make a man think twice, especially when he envisioned the sprawling army posts with their companies of troopers and shining cannons. But neither Wagner nor Grady was likely to make it that far, even if the big, heavily-muscled mules could keep ahead of the lighter, faster Indian ponies. Even pushing hard, Larned, the closer of the two posts, was a twenty-four hour ride.

Lifting the dun's reins, Clint said, "Let's go. We're going to have to push it now."

Lost His Horse slid his lathered pony to a halt above the crumbling cutbank of Rattlesnake Creek and leaped to the ground. The rawhide-wrapped stirrups of his elaborately quilled pad saddle flapped against the pony's flanks, but the animal was too winded to react. Warriors rose from the soft grass and deeper pockets of shade. They surrounded Lost His Horse, peppering him with questions. But the lanky warrior refused to be distracted. He pushed through the others and came to stand before Medicine Wolf.

"The white-eyes have left the spring. They ride toward the land of the Cree."

North, in the white man's tongue, toward the fort along the wagon road to Cherry Creek, the settlement they called Denver. Clenching his fists with impatience, Medicine Wolf waited silently for Lost His Horse to go on. He didn't trust himself to speak. His anger was like an evil spirit that had come to lodge in his breast; he could feel it writhing inside now, like a Mountain Devil, the wolverine whose ferociousness impressed even the cruelest among men.

Lost His Horse went on. "White Hawk is among them, but they are led by the man with the far-shooting gun. A woman is with them, and three who are wounded. Two of the mules are also wounded, and one will die before Sun comes again."

Medicine Wolf was suddenly puzzled. "You are sure of this?"

"Yes. I watched them leave."

Medicine Wolf turned away, walking to the steep bank of the creek and staring at the rippling flight of water bugs moving away from him, then darting rapidly to the side. He smiled with understanding, knowing that he had guessed wrong in assuming the white-eyes were trying to flee toward the pony-soldiers' fort on the road they called the Smoky Hill Trail. Like the water bug, their initial flight was only a ploy. Soon they would change directions, making a run for the stone lodge farther up the Rattlesnake. It impressed him that the man with the far-shooting gun was willing to risk the extra miles to trick them. It was something Coyote would think of, and it might have worked if Lost His Horse hadn't noticed the wounded mules.

"They will circle toward the land of the Arapaho, and seek shelter in the stone lodge," Medicine Wolf said softly.

Looks Far Man had been quiet during Lost His Horse's narration. Now he spoke up, puzzlement knitting his plucked brows. "Why would the white-eyes ride toward the

Cree hunting grounds if they wanted to go to the stone building?" Looks Far asked.

"To trick us. To make us look foolish. But we will not be fooled."

Yellow Knife stepped forward, his splinted arm cradled in his free hand. His face was a mask of hatred, his voice a pain-filled rasp. "Why do we worry about trickery? They are few in numbers, and we are many. Let us just go and kill them."

A chorus of assent rattled the drying leaves overhead. Medicine Wolf waited for it to die. The anger inside him had begun to settle now that the waiting was nearly finished. He shared Yellow Knife's passion, but a calm deliberateness had tempered his impatience. He said, "It is true that they are in the open. That is why we cannot forget the far-shooting gun. Yellow Knife is a brave man, but I think his arm has clouded his inside eyes. We cannot attack the whites-eyes in the open. We must think like Coyote. We must wait for them where they will not expect us, and kill them before any more die."

"But not the woman," Lost His Horse added suggestively. "We should not kill the woman too soon."

A ripple of coarse laughter greeted Lost His Horse's comment, but Medicine Wolf's expression never changed. "You may have the woman if you want her. It is White Hawk whom I seek. He must die for what he did on the Washita, but slowly, so that he understands the wrath of the People, and the price of his treachery."

"*Aiee,*" Looks Far growled, the laughter and smiles of the others dying away like an evening breeze. "We will not forget White Hawk."

They would have to act fast, though, Medicine Wolf knew. Already Sun was deserting the sky; it rested no more than a few hands above the horizon. He turned to face his friends, eyes narrowed in thought. "There is an arroyo where the valley comes close to the stone lodge. It is deep enough to cloak a man on horseback. White Hawk and the others must cross it if they follow the valley as far as the tall rock. I will ride hard to be there before they arrive. Who rides with me?"

There was an immediate volley of shouts, a general forward surge. Medicine Wolf smiled tightly. He had vowed that before the day was finished he would carry the head of the man who owned the far-shooting gun on his lance. It was time to go collect his prize.

CHAPTER 6

EMMA WILSON STOOD in the dappled shade of a cottonwood at the edge of the rambling grove that gave her father's station its name. Her arms were folded beneath her breasts, and the hot, dry wind molded the skirt of her calico dress to unadorned legs that had gone, in less than a year's time, from coltish to full and long. Her dark, wind-dulled hair was caught in a loose bun at the back of her neck in a way that made her feel plain. She had gray eyes, like her father's, and a small, pert nose she abhorred.

She stared westward along the L&P Cutoff. The road was empty, a shallow river of wind-eddied dust and hope, rippled by half-finished stories that swirled through the seasons of her life—unfinished because they belonged to other people's lives, those passengers and stray settlers or soldiers who passed through Cottonwood Station but never stayed. They went on, moving forever forward—east or west—to places where the lights burned all night and music floated along cobbled streets; where young people like herself danced and laughed, and maybe, if the moment was right, kissed in the silvery light of a full moon.

Emma had turned seventeen just recently. She day-dreamed of what it would be like to be kissed by a young man the way her father sometimes kissed her mother when they thought they were alone. Of course, she wouldn't want anyone patting her on the behind the way her father also did to her mother when they felt themselves unobserved, but maybe that would be okay after they were married.

She didn't know much about that, kissing and such.

41

There hadn't been much chance to learn, stuck out here in the middle of nowhere with no one really to talk to except her mother. About every third or fourth week a coach would hold over all night, the male passengers bunking with the hired man, Lester DeWeese, on curly buffalo robes in the storage room. But once in a while a woman came through and stayed the night as well, and if she didn't have a husband or look like she might be too friendly with the men—or used makeup—her mother would let her bunk in with Emma. Emma always looked forward to those times, especially when the women she bunked with wanted to talk. It was amazing the things a body could learn by reading between the lines, even from some of the older and more taciturn women. But it was those very women whose facade of properness allowed them to slip past her mother's scrutiny from whom Emma learned the most. Soiled doves, her mother would call them when she wanted to be polite.

Emma felt she would die before summer was over if she didn't escape the dreary desolation of the station. Her heart, which had started to wither from the unbearable emptiness of the plains, would never be able to stand another bleak and endless winter. She had to escape. She just had to.

She heard her little brother, Jack, shouting from the stable, where he was tagging after Lester DeWeese, who was twenty-two years old and smitten as ever an overly tall and gawky fool could be. Emma just knew the only reason Lester stayed on to work for her father was because he wanted to marry her. The thought made her so mad sometimes she just wanted to scream. She wasn't about to marry some snaggletoothed hayseed with horse apples for brains. At least her mother understood that, even if she did turn flustered, then angry, when Emma pushed for some kind of alternative.

For a while they had talked about Emma going back to

Ohio and living with her mother's sister, Carrie, who was married to a barber and had four fine, strapping sons. But her father had squashed that idea flatter than a stepped-on June bug. He wouldn't allow his little girl to live in the same house with four adolescent males. Such a notion was too far-fetched to even be discussed, and what could her mother do but agree.

That was why Emma had decided to run away on the next stage. That should've been the nine o'clock from Pueblo, with Greg Potts handling the lines. But the Colorado stage was running late, if it was running at all. Watching the empty road wistfully, Emma wondered if the Indian scare that had washed over the plains earlier that summer was flaring up again, frightening all the passengers off. She knew the company wasn't likely to schedule a run without paying customers.

Emma would have preferred going east, but she'd heard enough about Denver to figure that would do for a start. Maybe it would be smarter to take the later coach from Leavenworth, Amos Booth's rig. Amos's coach was running late today, too, and likely he'd be in a hurry once he rolled in, wanting to get the teams switched and the passengers fed and get back on the road to make up for whatever had slowed them down. That would mean he and her father wouldn't have much chance to talk, making it easier to bluff herself a seat on the rig when her parents thought she was in the kitchen, cleaning up. It occurred to her, almost as an afterthought, that it might also be nice to have Grady Shaw riding shotgun. She thought Grady might be a little sweet on her, too, and although he was also something of a clod sometimes, he seemed positively knightly when compared to Lester DeWeese.

Emma had it all figured out, the note ready to pin to her pillow, her valise and purse stashed in the weeds beside the stable. Just before the stage was ready to pull out she would slide out the back door while her mother and father were standing in front of the house talking to Amos, the way they always did. She would slip around to the stable and pick up her valise and enter the coach from the off side. With a little luck, and especially if it was dark (which was likely if Amos was much later getting in), no one would know about an extra passenger until the breakfast stop, well inside Colorado Territory. She wasn't sure what she would do then, but she was determined Amos wouldn't send her back. She was on her way, and nothing was going to stop her now.

The sun blazed into their eyes, blurring the western rim of the valley with its rays. The ridges to either side were crowned with caprock, slashed by jagged arroyos. Sprawling clumps of prickly pear spotted the slopes like faded green stains on a tan carpet.

Clint kept the dun to the middle of the valley, as far from the arroyos as he could get. Uneasiness gnawed at him. He kept shifting the Whitworth from the crook of his left arm to his saddlebows, then back again. His eyes, beneath the broad, low-pulled brim of his hat, flitted constantly.

He heard the belly-grunts of a jogging mule coming up from behind, but didn't stop. A moment later Kane reined in beside him. Amos Booth trotted up on the other side, his face a grimace of pain from the mule's jarring gait.

"You're leading us straight into a trap, sonny," Kane accused in a drawn voice. "By God, you know it, too, don't you? You kin feel it same as me."

"What's he talking about?" Booth demanded.

Clint nodded around them. "No antelope in sight, and the last buffalo I saw was an old bull trotting off to the north like something had spooked him." He pulled up, and the others ground to a halt around him, the mules snuffling and shaking their heads. "Kane's right. Something's wrong."

There was a groan from behind them, and Ruby called, "Clint." She slid to the ground and hurried to the stretcher's side.

Clint dismounted and let the dun's reins drag in the dusty grass. Booth also slid awkwardly from his mount, grunting when he hit the ground, staggering a little. "Christ," Kane muttered, shaking his head.

Grady was stirring, his head pivoting slowly in pain, while his knees lifted an inch or so to strain weakly at the straps holding him in place. He looked pale and clammy, his lips dry, caked with dust.

"I wish we had some water," Ruby said, brushing the damp hair back from Grady's forehead.

"How far are we from the station?" Clint asked Booth.

"Not more'n a couple miles." He nodded toward a jumbled pinnacle of caprock to the southwest, rising fifteen or twenty feet above the ridge supporting it. "I'd reckon that's the back of ol' Rocky Top there. The station'll be just on the other side."

One last barrier, Clint thought, eyeing the steep slopes that belled down from the tangle of rocks. Maybe the last chance the Cheyenne would get if they hadn't been duped by their ruse of swinging north first. His gut told him they hadn't, although he wasn't sure it mattered. Even if they hadn't fooled the Cheyenne for long, they'd probably kept the warriors guessing, buying themselves a little extra time and working their way that much closer. He lowered the Whitworth's breech, checked the huge brass shell chambered inside with the ball of his thumb, then slapped the trigger guard, levering the breech closed with the palm of his hand.

"You figure we ought to make a run for it?" Booth asked.

"Onliest thing we can do now," Kane interjected. His head was swiveling jerkily, his nostrils flaring.

Clint rested the Whitworth's heavy octagon barrel over

his shoulder. "Maybe, but we won't make a straight run. We're going to circle one more time."

"Circle!" Kane exploded. "Hell's fire, ain't you run us all over these hills long enough? You ain't gonna outfox them redskins, sonny. You might as well give up on that notion. They're gonna be one step ahead of you every step of the way. Best we just plow on through 'em right now and get it over with." He held his rifle up, as if he thought Clint had forgotten he carried it. Sunlight winked dully off the Henry's brass. "Fourteen shots, boys. This'll open a hole through 'em, by God."

Booth glanced at Clint, his eyes awash in indecision. Wagner looked on from atop the mule with grave countenance. Only Ruby revealed no hesitation in her steady gaze. She had placed her trust in Clint back at the stage, and it had become like a huge, deeply embedded stone, unmovable.

Clint stared at Rocky Top for several minutes, then shook his head. "No." He looked at Booth, explaining, "Even with fourteen rounds, Kane couldn't open a big enough path to get us all through. That Henry rifle of his hasn't got the range." He didn't add that his greatest doubt was of Kane's loyalty. He could only hope that Booth would already know that.

Grady stirred again, his tongue darting out to dab dryly at his lips. His eyelids fluttered, but didn't open. Ruby said, "We'd better do something. Traveling will be a lot harder on him after he wakes up."

"Let's ride," Clint said. He helped Ruby onto her mule, then turned to the dun, gathering the reins and swinging into the saddle. Kane glared at him with something akin to hatred, but Clint only nodded toward the ridge to the south, indicating the direction he wanted them to go. They would skirt Rocky Top well to the east, and come into Cottonwood Station from that direction.

Kane slapped his moccasined heels into the mule's

flanks and set off at a swift, ground-eating jog. Tugging on the stretcher mules' lead rope, Clint followed, glad to have Kane in front of him for a change. Amos Booth kept pace beside the stretcher, glancing worriedly down at his friend's pallid face from time to time, while Ruby flanked the young shotgun on the opposite side. The rough gait elicited a few moans from the stretcher, but that was all. They were almost to the base of the ridge when an arroyo snaking down from Rocky Top's crumbled skirt seemed to erupt with shrilly yipping savages. Ruby cried out in fright, and Wagner gasped, "My word!"

Twisting atop his mount, Kane's frantic gaze found Clint. "I told you, by God!" he screeched. "I told you!" He slammed the Henry's barrel against the base of his mule's tail, startling the animal into a jarring canter.

Clint threw the stretcher mule's lead rope over its neck and yelled, slapping the animal's hip with the loose ends of the dun's reins. Booth drew his revolver and fired a round into the dirt under the mule's belly. The mules broke into an awkward run, kicking and snorting at the stretcher's inflexible jerking. Clint reined his horse to Ruby's side. "Hang on," he shouted, and jabbed his spur into the mule's flank.

They raced toward the top of the ridge, the Cheyenne rolling toward them like a low brown wave. Clint held the dun back to create a slim, bobbing shield between the Indians and Ruby. On their faster ponies and crossing the slope at a gentler angle, the Cheyenne quickly closed the distance between the two groups. They were still a couple of hundred yards away when a rifle cracked from among the Cheyenne. The bullet tore up a chunk of sod several yards to the side and tossed it casually into the air. Kane, well in advance of the others, answered with the Henry, banging away wildly, peppering the sky or kicking up spirals of dust far in advance of the charging warriors.

Clint thumbed the Whitworth's hammer back to full

cock. He knew it would be futile to try to aim from the back of a running mount. Instead he chose his target—a big gray stud with lightning designs painted across its chest—and jerked the Whitworth to his shoulder, snapping his shot off instinctively. A splash of crimson appeared at the gray's shoulder, and it stumbled and fell, throwing its rider over its head. It was then Clint spotted the red and white Appaloosa, the one he'd last seen at the stage. It leaped the fallen gray effortlessly and edged toward the front of the churning mass of warriors. Grimly, Clint reloaded the Whitworth.

"We ain't gonna make it!" Booth shouted over his shoulder.

"Keep riding," Clint commanded without looking forward. His attention was focused on the Appaloosa now, and the tall, wiry war chief who rode it with the easy grace of a man born to the back of a horse. The Cheyenne's hair was long, black, unbraided, flowing on the wind like a silken veil. His skin gleamed like burnished copper in the slanting afternoon light, streaked with war paint. He carried an old muzzleloader in his hands; a war club dangled from his wrist like a grisly bracelet. His face looked hideous from a distance, an image enhanced by the black and yellow war paint that covered his chin and cheeks.

The Cheyenne gunfire increased. Arrows arched across the fading blue sky and thudded into the ground beside them, creeping gradually closer. A bullet whipped past Clint's ear with an angry, wasplike buzz. The Cheyenne were starting to veer toward the top of the ridge now, attempting to cut them off before reaching the crest. Kane emptied his rifle without having struck a single warrior, and began using it as a club against his mule's croup. Booth tried a shot with his revolver, but the Indians were still nearly eighty yards away, well out of revolver range.

Clint let his reins fall over the dun's pumping withers. He straightened in the saddle, rocking easily with the animal's gait. The Whitworth felt suddenly light in his hands, the way it often did when running buffalo. He let himself relax, let the fear and tension drain from his body. He stared at the warrior on the Appaloosa, pulling his concentration down until just the two of them existed.

He cocked the Whitworth, feeling the racheting slide of spring and sear through his thumb. He had missed his first chance back at the stage, but he wouldn't miss again.

But before he could shoulder the rifle, Ruby's mule squealed and grunted above the wet slap of lead striking flesh. Clint jerked around just as the mule's front legs buckled. Ruby cried out as the mule stumbled, kicking free of the tugs and pushing away from the falling animal. She fell hard, rolling in a tangle of green skirt and white petticoats, her red-gold hair pulling loose from its pins to lash the ground.

Clint swore and pulled the dun to a halt. Booth, herding the stretcher mules before him, and with Wagner clinging desperately to his belt, raced on unaware of what had happened. Kane, unhampered by any concern for the others, had quickly outdistanced them all, far enough ahead that he would easily beat the Cheyenne to the top of the ridge.

Alone, Clint whirled and slapped his spurs to the dun's flanks. Ruby was already scrambling to her feet, her eyes wide, searching. She spotted Clint and started to run toward him, Grady's revolver bouncing without notice on her hip.

Most of the Cheyenne continued after Kane, but a number of them veered their ponies away when they saw Ruby's mule fall. Clint slid the dun to a stop and threw the Whitworth to his shoulder. He found a brave in his sights and squeezed the trigger, his bullet slamming the warrior from the back of his mount.

"Clint!"

He lowered his hand. "Grab hold!"

She grasped his forearm, and Clint tightened his fingers around hers. She jumped, the pointed toe of her shoe catching the instep of Clint's foot behind his stirrup. He hauled her up behind him and spun his mount toward the Cheyenne. A bullet struck the pommel of his saddle, ripping away a chunk of leather and wood. An arrow whistled past, so close he thought he could feel the brush of its feathers. Dropping the Whitworth across his saddle-bows, Clint palmed his revolver.

"What are you doing?" Ruby asked shrilly.

"Hang on!" Clint returned, driving his spurs into the dun's ribs. The gelding lunged forward with a vigor that almost unseated Ruby. "Hold on," Clint shouted.

The Cheyenne were less than thirty yards away now, but Clint's offensive move caught them off guard. He raked the dun's flanks cruelly with his spurs; the horse squealed in anger and pain and laid its ears back. The Indians started to pull up, to break apart. There were seven of them, far too many to think of outfighting. But Clint didn't want to rout them. He only wanted to pass through, to break their charge and stop them long enough to give Ruby and him a chance.

"Clint! No!"

Clint snapped a shot toward the center of the group. An Indian cried out and grabbed his arm. Clint fired again, and a second warrior twitched and fell. The Indians split then, urging their mounts forward but sliding off the far sides to hang with only a heel and hand showing. Clint thrilled at the display of horsemanship in spite of the danger. The Cheyenne broke to either side of the dun like a river breaching an island. Gunfire ripped the air around the dun. Clint tasted the acrid tinge of gun smoke on the wind. Then they were through the Indians and running alone toward Rocky Top, the dun's hooves flashing over the ground. The Cheyenne immediately whipped their ponies around to follow.

Clint risked a glance toward the top of the ridge. Kane had already disappeared over the far side, leaving Booth and Wagner and the stretcher mules to make it on their own. But strangely, only a handful of Indians were chasing Booth, who had angled away from the path of Kane's flight. Most of the war party was streaking toward the top of the ridge after the old frontiersman, ignoring the rest of them.

Booth was looking behind him, searching for Clint and Ruby and acting as though he was willing to swing back if they needed help. Clint waved him on, then turned away, bending low over the dun's neck and urging him on. With the dun carrying double, the Cheyenne were once more quickly closing the gap.

Clint reined toward the top of the ridge. The dun's shoulders pumped furiously on the steepening slope, but its stride never faltered. They reached the top of the ridge and started down the far side. The Cheyenne raced after them, yipping angrily. Far below, Clint could see Kane streaking toward a grove of cottonwoods in the middle of a flat no more than a mile away. The stage road ran in from the left like a pale yellow ribbon. The main body of Cheyenne were still chasing Kane, but it was obvious they weren't going to catch up before he reached the trees unless a lucky shot brought him down. Booth and the stretcher mules had apparently started to swing wide, then decided to cut back sharply to the west. They would come in behind the main war party and, if luck stayed with them, would be able to slip into the trees while the warriors' attention was still on Kane. Clint pushed the big, rangy gelding a little harder, hoping to join Booth and ride in the rest of the way together.

Lifting his Colt to shoulder level, he let the dun have its head.

CHAPTER 7

IT TURNED A little cooler as the day began to ebb. Not enough to make a man think of digging for his jacket, but, with a steady breeze blowing out of the west, enough to appreciate. Not that Rusty was inclined to complain about what was beyond his control, like the heat, or the emptiness that had been gnawing at their bellies all day. He took what fate threw his way and tried to make the best of it. The breeze for instance, or the rabbit Clyde had killed back at the last crossing of the creek. It was only a cottontail, and more than likely they'd argue about how to split it between five half-starved men, but Rusty didn't doubt that he'd get his share, if not a little more. Even then it wouldn't be much, but it would ride a hell of a lot easier on his stomach than the jerky and hardtack they'd been living on the past few days.

Rusty straightened his slumped shoulders and tried to arch the kink from the small of his back. He'd been riding along for the past hour without paying much attention to his surroundings, as they all had, but now he perked up, rubbing his eyes with a thumb and forefinger. There was a trace of smoke curling above a scattering of cottonwood trees in the distance and, just visible from this angle, the corner of a stone building. Rusty's mouth started watering. Under different circumstances he might have given the place a wide berth, considering Iola's proximity, but he was hungry and already envisioning fatback and cornbread and maybe some fresh garden truck for variety, it being about that time of year. Thoughts of Clyde's rabbit had awakened a craving no single cottontail was ever going to satisfy.

He smiled, and was just about to tell himself that maybe their luck was changing after all, when he heard the echo of a rifle from the far side of the ridge to their north. Shorty jogged his mount alongside Rusty's pinto.

"What was that?" Shorty asked.

"A hunter," Rusty replied, moving his right hand back from the saddle horn to rest on his thigh, near his Colt. "Just some buffalo hunter killing his supper."

As if to mock his assurances, more gunfire crackled from the far side of the ridge.

"He sounds almighty hungry," Shorty observed dryly.

"Maybe it's Injuns," Clyde called from behind them, urging his horse closer.

Clyde had been worrying about redskins ever since they'd passed Pawnee Rock, Rusty thought irritably. Then that afternoon they'd come across a wrecked coach, with blood in the grass and a dead Indian lying several yards away with a gaping, fist-sized cavity blown in his chest. Frank had taken the Indian's scalp while the rest of them had ransacked the baggage left behind, helping them-selves to some clothing and odds and ends of jewelry. They hadn't found any money, or anything else of value.

"Likely the damn redskins took everything," Frank had said, to which Shorty had replied, "Frank, you are as dumb as a mule turd," before turning away without elaborating. Shorty had been in what Rusty referred to as his "killing mood" ever since Iola, and he probably wouldn't let up until he'd drawn blood.

Now Shorty was at it again, provoking Clyde this time with a mocking grin. "See, Clyde, it's a good thing you ain't ate all that much the last couple of days. You'd be shitting your pants right now if you had." He laughed. "Filling your boots with scared."

Clyde's face reddened, but he didn't say anything. He'd also recognized Shorty's mood.

"If that's a stage station up ahead, maybe we'd better hurry along," Abe suggested.

The sound of gunfire continued erratically, interrupted from time to time by the heavier boom of a large-bore rifle. A scowl crossed Shorty's face, and he turned away from Clyde. "That's a goddamn Whitworth," he said. "I heard that sound enough during the war to recognize it anywhere."

"A sniper's rifle?"

"A rifled musket," Shorty corrected. "One day a Yankee sniper pinned us down on the Tennessee River with one of those. Killed the lieutenant and sarge and a couple of the boys before the sun went down. We were holed up in a little crater where some cannon powder had exploded, with only a broken-up howitzer for protection. It was in the middle of an open field, so you couldn't make a run for it, and so goddamn hot and humid we like to died." His anger was building as he spoke, his dark, killer's eyes smoldering beneath knitted brows. "I'd like to find the bastard who's shooting that rifle and jam the barrel up his ass far enough to blow his tonsils out," Shorty finished darkly.

Frank snickered at the image, or maybe just to placate Shorty's mood. Rusty said, "There's a lot of Whitworths out there now. Not all of 'em were used by snipers."

Shorty turned his icy glare on Rusty. "Most of 'em were," he said in a voice that left no room for argument.

"They're getting closer," Clyde said.

Rusty gathered the pinto's reins prudently. The sound of gunfire was swelling rapidly now, drawing nearer the top of the ridge. "Let's mosey a little faster," he proposed, and lifted the pinto to a canter. They were still better than a mile from the station when a lone rider came pounding over the top of the ridge on a mule. Seconds later nearly a score of painted warriors swarmed over the ridge behind him.

"Sonofabitch!" Clyde cried in a strangled voice.

Rusty cursed and drove his spurs into the pinto's flanks. The wind caught his hat and pulled it off his head to hang against his shoulders. They fled down the road in a tight, dust-churning group, the animosity that had been building between them gone completely now. Other riders came over the ridge, whites and Indians alike, and in no particular order. Rusty caught a glimpse of a flagging, bright green skirt and even in his fear felt a stirring of interest. All three groups were racing frantically toward the station.

"We're going the wrong way," Shorty yelled, laughing.

Rusty whooped and grinned and took the pinto's reins in his teeth. He pulled his Colts but didn't cock them. The others drew their weapons as well, revolvers mostly, except for Clyde, who preferred a shotgun for close-up work. The lone rider and the larger group of Indians were already closing in on the station. Rusty nudged the pinto with his left knee, guiding the horse to the right to intercept the handful of whites sweeping in undetected behind the larger group.

Kane was till a hundred yards from the low stone building that was the heart of Cottonwood Station when a rifle boomed from a slot near the ceiling, spilling a Cheyenne from his pony.

More rifles opened up, and the larger war party swerved sharply to the west, abandoning the chase. Clint cut the dun toward the rear of the party, hoping to slip in behind them before the Cheyenne realized they were there. Booth, still driving the stretcher mules before him, came in on Clint's left. Then, through dancing veils of dust, Clint spotted a knot of riders coming off the stage road toward them. Even as he watched, they opened up on the warriors still trailing Booth and Wagner, the sound of their revolvers crackling in the evening air.

"Hang on," Clint called to Ruby, digging at the dun with his spurs. The Indians who had been closing in on them from the rear began to falter. One of the Indians cried out and dropped his bow; another jerked convulsively and fell forward across his pony's neck. As if on cue, the rest broke away from the chase, splitting off to join the larger party.

Booth "yeehawed" as he lashed the stretcher mules toward the station, and the riders from the road, led by a short, powerfully built young man with long, curly red hair, swung in beside them. "Let's go!" the curly-haired man shouted past the reins clenched in his teeth. "They're coming back!"

Clint glanced to his right, seeing that the larger party had indeed stopped and rolled back on itself. The stragglers who had been following him and Booth joined them—thirty or more warriors altogether. But they had lost time in swerving aside, then turning back. Cottonwood Station beckoned from less than two hundred yards away, and Clint remembered Booth's description: *I doubt a cannonball would do more'n raise a little dust.*

From here, Clint was inclined to agree.

He bent low over the dun's neck. The gelding was breathing heavily now, but still running strong. Around the cinch strap a grimy lather appeared that was whipped back by the wind and the rhythm of the horse's pounding gait, spotting Clint's trouser legs. The little group raced toward the station while the Cheyenne closed in on their right, edging slightly ahead in an effort to cut them off before they could pass within the covering fire of the station. For a moment it looked like they might succeed. Then a volley of rifle fire opened from the station; powder smoke unfurled like dingy gray banners from crevices within the stone. A pair of Cheyenne tumbled from their ponies, and a bay flipped head over heels, throwing its rider clear.

The Cheyenne charge floundered, then came on, but they had lost their momentum. The whites reached the shade of the trees and pounded toward the station. The Cheyenne followed into the trees, but the deadly fire from the station finally broke their attack, driving them back into the sunlight. They retreated with angry whoops and curses flung at the station in choppy English, no doubt learned from soldiers or traders.

Clint pulled the heaving dun to a halt and slid from the saddle. Ruby followed, sobbing softly as she collapsed against him. Her cheeks were red and streaked with tears, her hair a matted snarl. Clint pulled her behind the protection of the dun and wrapped an arm around her trembling shoulders while he peered over the top of the saddle.

The Cheyenne had pulled back, but they hadn't given up. They raced back and forth across the sunlit flat, yelling taunts and flashing obscenities with fingers and hands. Now and again one would make a dash forward, but rifle fire from the narrow gun slots high in the station's walls always drove him back.

Clint pushed Ruby away gently, then slid the Whitworth's long barrel over the seat of his saddle. He thumbed a fresh cartridge into the breech, then flipped the vernier sight up and adjusted it to three hundred and fifty yards. He steadied the dun with a soothing patter of words as he searched the warriors sprinting chaotically across the flat. He looked first for the warrior on the Appaloosa, but when he couldn't find him in the dust and confusion, he chose a warrior on a bay instead, leading the Indian by half a pony's length as he squeezed the trigger. The Indian was jerked from the back of his pony, tumbling brokenly across the dusty grass. Clint quickly reloaded, but the Cheyenne had already had a taste of the Whitworth's accuracy. They began to pull back for good, their yelling and taunting tapering off. Clint watched silently with his thumb on the Whitworth's hammer. Quietly now, the Cheyenne climbed the ridge to the north and, one by one, disappeared over the top.

"That was some shooting," the curly-haired man said, leading a short-coupled pinto forward and extending his hand. "Best I've ever seen with a rifle."

Clint pulled the Whitworth back and folded the vernier down along the rifle's wrist. He glanced at the twin Colts holstered butts-forward at the stranger's waist, the stain on the walnut grips almost worn away with use. The man wore a flat-crowned, flat-brimmed black hat, dark striped trousers, and a soiled white shirt beneath a black and white cowhide vest. His spurs were made of silver and blue steel, with tiny jingle-bobs that *chinged* musically when he walked.

Clint took his hand, but couldn't force a smile. "Thanks," he said briefly.

The stranger turned his attention to Ruby, white teeth flashing. "A right rowdy ride, wasn't it, ma'am?"

"It seems we owe you our thanks as much as we do Mr. Dawson here," she said, sniffing and dabbing at her eyes. "You saved our lives."

The stranger looked momentarily confused. Then he laughed. "Why, I reckon we did then, didn't we? But we were glad to do it, too. It's always an honor to come to the aid of a pretty lady."

Ruby seemed to stiffen at the compliment, and her mouth slid into a rigid line.

Clint said, "This is Ruby Jennings, a passenger on the L&P. They had some trouble back down the road, and had to take the long way around. I'm Clint Dawson."

"Rusty Cantrell," the stranger replied. "I saw the stage laying on its side a ways back."

"We're lucky you happened along," Clint said.

"I would say," Rusty agreed, smiling cockily. "Looked like you folks were about to get your tail feathers plucked for sure."

"It wasn't the first time today the Cheyenne have tried to 'pluck us,' " Ruby said stiffly. "We've managed so far."

Rusty's smile broadened, the crow's-feet around his eyes deepening into tiny crevices. "Why, I reckon you're right, ma'am. And me and the boys, we do appreciate your kindness in letting us ride in with you." He bowed slightly to Ruby, nodded to Clint, then spun away, his heavily roweled spurs jingling.

"You know him?" Clint asked, puzzled, after Cantrell had walked out of earshot.

"I know his kind," Ruby answered curtly.

Booth came up, leading his sweat-darkened riding mule, with Wagner slumped above the withers, in one hand, the stretcher mules in the other. The lead stretcher mule was swaying on its feet, its shoulder glistening with blood pumping from the arrow wound it had picked up in the Cheyenne attack on the stage. "Reckon we'd best get these two unloaded," Booth said. "It ain't lookin' too promising right now." He glanced at Wagner. "Jerome started spitting blood on the way in, but there wasn't a damn thing I could do about it."

"Of course not," Ruby said quickly. She went to Wagner's side and put a hand on his knee. "Mr. Wagner? Can you hear me? Mr. Wagner?"

Booth looked at Clint and shook his head. A heavy wooden door creaked open near the center of the north wall, and a tall, gaunt man with a lantern jaw and hard gray eyes stepped outside. He carried a Sharps carbine in his left hand, muzzle dipped toward the ground. A revolver in a flapped cavalry holster was belted at his waist. He nodded to Clint, tipped a battered slouch hat to Ruby, then looked at Booth and spoke in a dry, graveled voice: "Amos."

"Hello, John." They shook hands, then Booth jerked his thumb toward Clint. "Clint Dawson. Clint, this is John Wilson, the station manager." They nodded again, and spoke, then Booth introduced Ruby and motioned toward Wagner. "Consumption, John. This man is needin' some help mighty bad. So is young Grady—he took a blow to his skull some time back."

Wilson glanced at the bandage and the dried blood on Booth's shoulder, then leaned his carbine against the wall. "Polly! Emma!" he called into the darkened interior. Looking at Booth, he said, "We'll care for the wounded first, and you can introduce the others and fill me in on the rest later." He took the stretcher mule's lead, wincing unconsciously when he saw the blood on the animal's shoulder, then led it closer to the door where a couple of women had hesitantly appeared. Leaving his dun to fend for itself momentarily, Clint went to help.

CHAPTER 8

A HEAVY SILENCE settled over the dusty flat fronting the station. The sun hung just above the horizon, low enough to peek beneath the rambling branches of the cottonwoods and throw its brassy light against the west wall of the station.

Clint climbed the gentle slope behind the station and stood atop the sod roof of the stable, the Whitworth heavy in his right hand.

Wilson had chosen his site well, Clint decided as he studied the layout. The trees would provide a smattering of wood and plenty of shade in the summer, as well as a decent windbreak during the winter. Cottonwood Creek wound sinuously through the grove, with several broad but shallow pools carved out of its bed with pick and shovel. The water there looked cool and clear, but there was also a well dug between the creek and the station for good measure, with a cross-beam overhead and a solid oak floor stout enough to hold a mule, but without walls that might hide a man.

The stable had been built into the side of the slope behind the station, a half dugout with everything canted forward and exposed to the rifle slots built into the main building. The walls inside the stable had been framed with lumber and whitewashed, eliminating shadows that might conceal an enemy. There was a large, three-railed corral to the side, one corner dipping into the creek around its lower pool. The upper end connected to a smaller corral that included the stable.

But it was the station itself that impressed Clint most. It

was a low, flat-roofed building with stone walls at least a foot and a half thick. A pair of slim bastions rose above the roof at opposite corners, one to the northwest, the other to the southeast. The bastions were encircled by rifle slots that offered a clear view of the station walls and roof, but gave nothing in return.

Rifle slots also lined the main building, placed about eight feet above the ground on the outside. On the inside there were narrow platforms hinged into the stone walls that a man could lower and stand on, and a shallow cavity to lean into and peer outside. The slots, like the two high windows on each wall, were protected by heavy, oak shutters on iron hinges, studded on the outside, as were the two doors, with nails to resist fire or the blade of an axe.

There were five rooms inside—a main room and kitchen that took up the west side of the building and was used to accommodate L&P passengers, a couple of bedrooms—one large and airy, used by Wilson and his stocky, stern-faced wife, and the other narrow and dark, as if partitioned off as an afterthought for their daughter, Emma. A large storage room on the southeast corner also had bunks to quarter the hired man, Lester DeWeese, and Wilson's somber-faced son, Jack. As an extra precaution, Wilson had dug a second well inside the station, near the northwest bastion.

It was, Clint thought as his gaze admiringly swept the grove and beyond, about as defensible a position as any he had ever seen. Yet no place was totally impenetrable, and he'd already spotted a number of vulnerable locations around the station; nothing major, but places where a couple of men could find a little cover and give them some trouble. Plus there were the trees that surrounded the station on all sides, with their sprawling, leaf-shrouded limbs and broad, knotty trunks. Nothing ideal, even for a skulking Cheyenne who could find cover behind a tick, but they would all bear watching.

Clint could hear Lester DeWeese in the stable beneath him, caring for the wounded stock. They had penned the mules, those Booth and the others had ridden in on, plus the fresh mules that had been waiting to replace the original team, along with Clint's dun and packhorse and the mounts of Cantrell's men in the small corral in front of the stable. The wounded mules had been stabled separately inside, where the other animals wouldn't chouse them. Clint doubted if either mule would live, but Wilson wanted to give them a chance.

"Do what you can for them," he'd told DeWeese. Then, revealing a more practical side, added, "If you can't save them, we'll butcher them."

Dragging his gear inside earlier and storing it in one of the bastions, Clint had noticed nearly a dozen smoked buffalo hams and an assortment of tongues hanging from the rafters that supported the upper platform. Airtights of tomatoes, peaches, apples, and other fruits and vegetables, plus sacks of dried peas, beans, flour, and corn filled the storeroom. But even with full stores, Wilson apparently wasn't a man to waste food, especially when no one knew how long they might be holed up here.

Clint fished a stubby white clay pipe and a sack of tobacco from a quilled bag at his belt. He fussed absently with it now, the Whitworth cribbed across his arm and his gaze slowly roaming the tall-grassed grove of trees. He could feel the tension draining out of him, a load like sand bags lifting from his shoulders. Without word or gesture, the responsibility he'd assumed for these people back at the wrecked coach had been shifted to Wilson's shoulders, and Clint was glad to be free of the burden.

Still, the freedom wasn't complete. The Cheyenne hadn't shown themselves since being driven over the ridge more than an hour before, but Clint knew they were still out there, regrouping. They'd taken a hell of a beating today—more killed or wounded than common sense could account for—and they'd want their revenge. The question was, how would they attempt it? Cheyenne were horse Indians, and it was hard to imagine them trying to slip in on foot, although that would have been their smartest move, considering the strength of the station and the number of armed men inside.

Booth had worried that the Cheyenne might try to smoke them out. The grass was dry enough, and the thick, roiling clouds of smoke from a prairie fire would more than likely stampede the stock into breaking down the corral and fleeing, a tempting reward for their effort no matter what results they garnered at the station itself. It would also offer a fair cover while they slipped in closer. But a scorched prairie burned for a long time after the flames went out, and Clint doubted many Cheyenne would be willing to risk crippling their ponies by blistering the frogs of their hooves. They would be even less likely to want to burn their own feet on the smoldering grass.

No, Clint decided. The Cheyenne were horse Indians, and they would fight as such. Pride would demand that much.

He glanced westward with a sudden tightening in his chest, a sudden instinctive knowing. They would make another attempt before darkness fell, and they would come from the west, where there sun's blinding light would shield them until they were close enough to overwhelm the station.

Amos Booth and John Wilson huddled in conversation in front of the station. Booth looked up as Clint approached, his face drawn with pain, shoulders sloped. He motioned Clint over. "Greg Potts is late on his eastbound run," Booth said. "We're thinkin' maybe the Cheyenne stopped him as well."

"It's possible," Clint acknowledged. He glanced at Wilson, regarding the quiet station manager thoughtfully.

Wilson was something of an enigma. Despite his worn, baggy dress of overalls, sweat-stained hickory shirt, heavy brogan shoes, and old, shapeless hat, there was something in the man's eyes that didn't quite fit the role of a bedraggled innkeeper and stage hostler. The oddity of his raising a family this far west also made Clint wonder. Generally a man with a wife and kids dug in closer to the settlements, unless he was either a fool or a sonofabitch who just didn't care what risk he put his family in. John Wilson didn't seem like either.

"John wants to send a man to Fort Larned for help," Booth said. "He figures Potts could be stranded out there same as we were."

Clint shifted his weight from one foot to the other, already sensing Wilson's line of reasoning. "Who do you want to send?" he asked finally.

"You or Kane," Wilson said evenly. "And Amos doesn't trust Kane."

A smile broke the stiff countenance of Clint's features. "Neither do I. Give Kane a good horse and a head start and he'll go his own way and never mention the ones he left behind. But I won't go."

Wilson's eyes narrowed suspiciously. "You don't look like a coward, Dawson. Maybe I'm wrong."

"That won't work either," Clint replied. He paused, then went on. "It's too risky to send a rider out now. They'll be watching us too close for a while. But that won't last. They'll pester us for a couple of days, probably make a try for the stock, but we can hold out as long as we're careful. There's enough food and plenty of water, and with Cantrell's bunch we've got the guns." Wilson's brows pulled into a vee at mention of Cantrell, but Clint continued without pause. "If Potts is out there, he's either dead by now or on his way in . . . here or somewhere else. Assuming he even left Pueblo."

Wilson seemed to consider Clint's words carefully, his

hard gray eyes revealing nothing. Finally he said, "You may be right, for the time being. But you need to understand that this is my station, Mr. Dawson, and if I decide to send a man to Larned, he'll go."

Clint's smile turned brittle. "You were a military man then?"

"I was. In an artillery outfit under General Meade, at Gettysburg."

"An officer?"

"A major," Wilson said in a strangely reflective tone. "It was a field commission earned at Chancellorsville."

"I'm not one of your soldiers, Wilson, and I've fought Indians before. Give them a day or two and they'll ride off looking for easier prey."

"I'll give them until tomorrow afternoon. If they haven't pulled out by then I'll have to reconsider sending for help, no matter what the risk to the rider."

"They'll try again," Clint said bluntly. He motioned toward the western end of the grove, where the sun's light seemed to diffuse visibility. "Before sundown. We'd best be ready for them."

Wilson nodded gently as he studied the far trees. "You have a point," he said. "Let's go inside and prepare for them."

DeWeese came shambling from the stable, wiping salve from his fingers with a burlap rag. He was a tall, gangling youth with rumpled hair and placid expression, forever looking to the ground. Although he wore much the same outfit as his employer—clumsy brogan shoes, faded overalls, worn shirt, and a shapeless hat—he seemed more at home in such dress.

"Have you fed and watered all the stock?" Wilson asked with what appeared to be an accepted patience.

"Uh-huh."

"The wounded stock too?"

"Yep. They ain't ever gonna pull a coach agin, but might be the number two'll pull through. He ain't bad atall."

"Good. Is everything secured? Gates latched and pad-locked?"

"Tighter'n a tick's ass," DeWeese replied.

"Then let's get inside," Wilson said, glancing to the west, where the buttery flood of light was already fading.

The station's interior was dark and cool after the fiery brightness of a Kansas summer afternoon. The shutters were pulled shut and bolted, adding to the cavernous atmosphere. A couple of lamps were burning around the main room, and Wilson's wife and daughter were putter-ing in the yellow glow of a third lamp in the kitchen. The smell of bubbling stew filled the room with a tantalizing aroma, stirring Clint's hunger.

Rusty Cantrell and his men sat at the long plank table that formed a partition between the main room and the kitchen. Three of them were playing poker with a new-looking deck, using cartridges for chips. Cantrell sat in a straight-backed chair at the head of the table, his legs stretched before him and crossed at the ankles. He was watching the women as they worked in the kitchen, but looked around when Clint, Booth, and Wilson entered the station. Kane and Cantrell's fourth man, the dark, silently morose gunhand named Aaron, were keeping watch in the bastions. Wilson's boy, Jack, sat quietly at the far end of the table, watching the men play cards.

Grady Shaw and Jerome Wagner had been put to bed in the larger of the two bedrooms. Clint had looked in on them earlier. Wagner was either deeply asleep or uncon-scious. His breathing was quick and shallow, accompanied by a hoarse rattling and a trace of blood at the corner of his mouth. But Grady was showing definite signs of com-ing around, groaning and kicking weakly at his blankets, his head pivoting as if in a dream.

Ruby sat alone in a rocker between the fireplace and the

door leading to the wounded men's bedroom, and Clint went to her side in pretense of knocking the dottle from his pipe. Squatting beside the hearth, he began picking at the bowl with an antler-tipped brass wire. "How are you holding up?" he asked quietly.

She gave him a grudging smile. "Fine, for a second-class citizen." At Clint's cocked brows, she nodded toward the kitchen. "The lady of the house has her bun pulled a little too tight. It's drawn her nose into the air."

Clint chuckled, giving the pair in the kitchen a glance. Polly Wilson was a broad-hipped, austere-looking woman with graying hair and a sharp nose. She looked as solid and unflappable as a good Missouri mule and handled her utensils with a clattering efficiency.

The daughter, Emma, showed little of her mother's stern qualities. She was helping with only half her attention focused on the job at hand, fluttering around and bumping into her mother, getting in the way as much as she helped, it seemed. Her gaze kept wandering toward Cantrell, then darting away, obviously as flustered by the young gunman's unabashed stare as she was intrigued. She was attractive but young, and probably immature, Clint decided.

"That bastard," Ruby said in a low-keyed anger.

"Don't worry about Cantrell," Clint murmured. He put his pipe away and stood. "He'll be too busy in a couple of minutes to think about flirting with girls."

Ruby looked around the room, noticing for the first time that Wilson and Booth had also disappeared into the bastions. An alarmed expression crossed her face.

"It may be nothing," Clint said. He glanced again at Cantrell's men, heartened by the familiar ease with which they carried their weapons, their relaxed manner. They were men created by war, honed to a natural and constant vigilance, yet able to face danger with an air of nonchalance that Clint envied. He was glad to have them, regardless of Wilson's distrust. He gave Ruby a reassuring smile and turned toward the northwest bastion.

It was cramped inside the dark, circular room. Standing in the center, Clint could have easily touched both sides of the stone walls. He stared up the peeled cottonwood ladder, past the red-tinged buffalo hams that hung from the rafters like smoked Christmas ornaments. Wilson stood on the top rung, peering over Kane's white-mantled shoulder through a rifle slot. Kane was crouched on a narrow wooden platform with his Henry rifle cradled across his lap.

"Anything?" Clint asked.

Kane glanced down, an expression bordering on hatred twisting his features. "Be redskinned devils soon enough, Dawson," he snarled. "Somebody oughta go for help, before them bastards steal our horses."

"You, no doubt," Clint answered dryly.

"I'm the best man for the job, you damn right. The only man here who'd stand a snowball's chance in hell of getting through."

Clint's anger swelled at last. "Through to where, Kane? The nearest saloon?"

Kane tried to turn, but it was too crowded with Wilson at his shoulder. "What are you gettin' at, sonny? Spit it out, 'cause I'm gettin' tired of your hintin' around all the time."

"Better save it for later," Wilson commanded sharply, stifling Clint's reply. "Here they come!"

CHAPTER 9

THEY CAME FROM the west, as Clint had predicted, splintering at the edge of the trees like shattered glass. Except for the rolling thunder of their ponies' hooves drumming the grassy carpet, they came silently, hoping for surprise.

Clint leapt atop the rifle platform and slid the Whitworth's long barrel through the vertical slot. He already had a shell chambered. He thumbed back the hammer, not bothering with the vernier sight. At this range the rifle's standard ladder sight would work just as well.

Cantrell and his men scrambled for the positions that Wilson had assigned earlier. Rusty and Shorty Phelps helped Clint, Wilson and Kane covered the west wall, while the others scattered to other rooms, other walls. Kane's Henry rattled turbulently from the bastion, his shots as wild from a moored platform as they had been from the back of a bolting mule.

Wilson's carbine roared, spinning a Cheyenne from the back of his pony. Clint steadied the Whitworth and dropped a second warrior. But the remaining Cheyenne pressed mulishly forward, swooping under the sprawling limbs like barn swallows. Clint hurriedly reloaded and fired again, then set the Whitworth aside and pulled his Colt.

As the Indians came closer, Cantrell and Phelps opened up with their revolvers, raking the front line of warriors with lead. One rider, then two were spilled from the backs of their ponies. The deadly hail cleaved the Cheyenne charge like a leaden axe, and as they split around the squat stone building the others opened up on them from the sides. Clyde Cooper's shotgun boomed twice, and Emma and Polly Wilson's Springfields each cracked a shot. DeWeese held the north wall with a stubby Spencer, while Booth and Ruby held the back wall.

The din inside the station hammered Clint's ears painfully. Powder smoke stung his eyes and seared the back of his throat. He jumped down from the platform as soon as the last Cheyenne passed from sight and grabbed the Whitworth, hurrying into the bigger bedroom, where Grady and Wagner rested unconcerned. Ruby stood at the corner slot where she could cover both directions, Grady's smoking revolver held in both hands. She looked around when Clint approached, a relieved expression loosening the muscles of her face.

"They're leaving," she said, her words almost lost in the ringing in Clint's ears. "We've driven them off."

She was right. By the time full darkness fell a couple of hours later, the Cheyenne hadn't returned.

It was obvious now that Man Above had betrayed him.

Medicine Wolf sat on the side of a wind-scoured hill and stared through the darkness at his moccasins—moccasins Red Willow Woman had made for him last summer while his band of the People hunted buffalo along Sand Creek. They had camped less than a day's ride from the site where Black Kettle was betrayed by the whites the first time, his village along Sand Creek destroyed by the man called Chivington. Medicine Wolf had ridden past that fateful spot one afternoon late last summer. It had been a hot day, and he remembered vividly the purpling clouds far to the west, sweeping the distant horizon with veils of rain.

Looks Far Man, Yellow Knife, and Running Elk had come with him, but they'd refused to wander through the site as Medicine Wolf had. They hadn't chided him for his decision to explore the sacred spot, but he had seen the dismay in their eyes as he'd reined his pony away from them. They hadn't wanted to offend the spirits who remained behind, Medicine Wolf knew, but he hadn't worried about such protocol. He wanted to see the place where so many of his mother's brothers and their families had died.

Only a few old lodge poles and some scattered bones remained, pitted with decay and nearly grown over with grass. Everything else had been reclaimed by their Mother, the earth.

A feeling of bleak desolation filled Medicine Wolf as he wandered slowly across the sun-cracked land. Even with the grass and the heat-curled leaves of a couple of stunted cottonwood trees, the place had seemed foreboding, without life. The feeling of lifelessness nagged at Medicine Wolf as he walked along the sandy bank of the creek, causing his scalp to crawl. He began to feel like an intruder. Yet he willed himself to stay, telling himself that this place was claimed by Cheyenne spirits and was friendly toward him.

He knew now that he had been wrong, and that Man Above was punishing him for his transgression. In the Season of the Yellowing Leaves He had given Medicine Wolf a wife and made her fertile. Then, just as she had begun to swell with child, He had snatched her away from him. He had left her nubile form twisted grotesquely in death along the icy banks of the Washita for Medicine Wolf to discover, mutilated by Custer's Osage scouts.

Then the grass turned green and Sun traveled back north to visit the land of the People. Man Above made Medicine Wolf a war chief of Blue Man Limping's village, giving him friends who believed in his skills and powers, and who had followed him faithfully on his journey north to find the traitor, White Hawk. The man called Kane by the white-eyes.

Now Man Above dangled White Hawk just out of his

reach, a tantalizing bait that had already lured too many of Medicine Wolf's brothers to their deaths.

Medicine Wolf jerked his head back, the muscles in his throat pulled taut. He wanted to scream, but Man Above had not yet broken him that far. Even though he grieved for Red Willow Woman, for Lone Bull and Hump and Ugly, and the others who had died this day by the rifles of the unholy whites, Medicine Wolf would not allow himself to grovel, not even before Man Above.

He was of the People, a warrior.

Fighting back the agony of loss, he calmed himself. Tomorrow they would fight again. Tomorrow they would tear down the stone lodge where the fox, White Hawk, hid and have their revenge against those inside.

Rusty Cantrell tipped a ladder-back chair into the cool stone of the inner wall and hooked his heels on the well-worn rungs. Fishing a bag of Lone Jack and his smoking papers from a vest pocket, he began to fashion a cigarette. Alone and unwatched, he lowered his guard enough to use both hands to roll his smoke. He worked slowly, shaping the stubby cigarette with a single-minded deliberateness, and when he was finished he held it up to the light of a nearby lamp, examining it critically. A smile creased his face. There was a slight wrinkle next to the seam, but Rusty figured he could live with that. He'd become used to living with small imperfections over the years.

Rusty was twenty-eight, an age that surprised him not so much for the years behind him, but for those still ahead. He was occasionally amazed by the amount of living he'd managed to cram into less than three decades.

He'd run away from home when he was twelve, getting a jump on life, he supposed. He went to St. Louis first, walking all the way and hoping to find work as a clerk or an accountant, being handy with figures. He wasn't fast but he was accurate, the only one in his family who could multiply and divide in fractions.

But jobs were scarce and wages were poor. When he couldn't find work clerking he began to steal . . . pies off windowsills, hams out of backyard smokehouses, watermelons and sweet corn and such out of gardens. He got a job mucking stables near the riverfront and hoarded his meager earnings as much as possible.

When the leaves began to change colors in the fall he stole a jacket off a clothesline, some heavy wool shirts out of a store, and a new pair of boots. A clerk caught him stealing the boots, but a well-placed kick to the man's groin afforded Rusty's escape. The next day a constable showed up at the stable, looking for him, but Rusty burrowed into a stack of hay and waited him out. That night he broke into the stable office and stole a flat tin box containing some cash, a cheap pocket watch, and a .42-caliber pepperbox pistol. By dawn he was forty miles down the Mississippi River in a stolen skiff.

His luck ran hot and cold over the next few years. He did a little time in the county jail in Evansville, Indiana, and got the hell beat out of him by a sheriff outside Cannelton, of the same state. When he was eighteen he put together a gang of hooligans ranging in age from eleven to sixteen, and made a foray through the northern Kentucky countryside, stealing horses and burning barns just for the hell of it. They broke into a few homes and destroyed whatever they didn't steal. They waylaid a tobacco broker between Frankfort and Lexington and relieved him of nearly four thousand dollars in cash and a diamond-studded pocket watch to replace the cheap one Rusty had taken from the stable in St. Louis.

They had a hell of a good time for a while. Then a posse caught up with them near Bardstown.

He met Clyde Cooper in the state penitentiary outside Louisville and spent three years bunking with him on the second tier, cell 224. Clyde got out six months before Rusty, but hung around Louisville working on the quays. Once Rusty hit town they stole some revolvers and Clyde stole his first shotgun, then they spirited a couple of good Kentucky thoroughbreds off a plantation south of town and made a run for Indiana.

Luck rode with them all the way this time. South Carolina had seceded from the Union just before Christmas, and within weeks six other states followed suit. The South fired on Fort Sumter two days before Rusty's release, and Louisville was in an uproar of divided loyalties. After decades of clumsy maneuvering and last-ditch compromises, the nation had slid pell-mell into war, and no one much gave a damn about a couple of horse thieves on the lam toward Indiana.

They went back to Missouri, where they joined some bald-knobbers in rooting out Union sympathizers and copperheads. Mostly they looted the Unionists' homes and barns, and sold what they confiscated on the black market that quickly sprang up around the bigger cities. Very little of what they stole actually went into Southern coffers, but the rhetoric of "The Cause" attracted a lot of grassroots support.

Occasionally they hanged someone who refused to see the intelligence of their arguments, and once in a while they hanged someone who did agree with them, but had maybe ticked one of the gang off somehow. It was a rough bunch all right, and Rusty wasn't all that sorry when most of them were captured by the Union Army toward the end of the war and hanged, four at a time, at the Jefferson City gallows.

Rusty, Clyde, and Abe Aaron, who'd joined them in Missouri, went up to Iowa and turned honest for a summer. Lord knew they had the money for it by then. They bought a herd of cattle and drove them up to Minnesota, where they made a tidy but boring profit, then returned to Missouri and crime. It wasn't as safe as dealing in cattle, but it was a lot more fun.

Shorty Phelps joined them the April Bob Lee surrendered at Appomattox, and Frank Cassidy rounded out the gang to a manageable number a couple of months later. A hotheaded ex-raider named Cole Younger rode with them for a while, then decided the Cantrell bunch was too tame for his taste. Rusty was inclined to agree; Cole Younger was like a smoldering ball of anger sputtering rapidly toward explosion, and Rusty was glad to see him go.

They started hitting banks, railroads, mine payroll offices, and stagecoaches on a regular basis, keeping it small-time and never striking in the same place twice. When possible, they tried to shift the blame onto the Reno brothers out of central Indiana or the James gang that was just getting started in Missouri. The Renos and the Jameses seemed to thrive on the notoriety, whereas Rusty was content with a more uninspiring career.

It was a good life while it lasted, but Rusty always knew it would have to end someday. Iola and a couple of laughing kids with straw-colored hair had marked its end.

Rusty struck a match on the stone wall and lit his cigarette. It was late, and most of the others were already in bed. He could hear Clyde and Abe snoring in the storage room. The old frontiersman, Kane, was rolled up in a buffalo robe near the front door. DeWeese kept an early watch in the northwest bastion, while Frank manned the southeast corner. Clint Dawson, John Wilson, and Shorty had taken their bedrolls outside to sleep in the open, where they could keep an eye on the stock. It made Rusty want to chuckle to remember Shorty following the other two outside. Ol' Shorty was a great one for proving no one was tougher than he was. Rusty figured that if he had anything to prove personally, it wasn't that he could sleep through some redskin slipping up on him in the middle of the night and cutting his throat.

The door to the middle bedroom swung quietly open, and Ruby Jennings came out, wearing a baggy robe buttoned high around her neck, but too short to reach her ankles. Rusty caught a glimpse of ruffled petticoats beneath the robe's hem and let his chair down softly, yet with enough of a click on the wooden floor to draw her attention. Ruby froze as if discovered in something illicit, then nodded curtly when she recognized him, and pulled the door shut behind her. She made her way barefooted to the corner bedroom where the wounded men slept, shutting the door after her.

Rusty drew on his cigarette, regarding the closed door thoughtfully for several minutes. Then a smile tipped the corner of his mouth, and he threw his cigarette into the fireplace. He was aware of Kane's eyes following him across the room, but didn't much care what that old fool was thinking. So far as Rusty was concerned, the best way to deflate an old blowhard like Kane was to just ignore him.

Ruby was bent over one of the men when Rusty entered, her wrist pressed lightly to his forehead. She looked up, her eyes widening in alarm, but didn't shout. Grinning, Rusty heeled the door shut and leaned against it. A lamp burning on top of a chest of drawers against the far wall threw its dim light over the double bed, striking Ruby's red-gold hair like spun threads.

Ruby straightened and nervously smoothed the pleated flow of her robe. She had cleaned up earlier, scrubbing the trail dust and smudges of powder smoke from her face, and combing her hair into a loose bun that rested against the back of her neck. Despite the ragged appearance of her dress and a haggard cast to her face, she looked beautiful to Rusty, who had been without a woman for almost two weeks.

"How are they?" he asked, nodding toward the sleeping men.

Ruby moved away from the bed as if reluctant to disturb

their sleep, yet cautious too, keeping her distance. Rusty's grin widened, catlike.

"I think Grady's sleeping now," the woman said. "He came to for a little while just before the Cheyenne attacked the last time. I gave him some water and he spoke a few words. He'll be okay with time."

"Well, that's good," Rusty said, taking a step closer and lowering his voice. Ruby lifted her chin defiantly.

"My, my," Rusty said in mock wonder. "I always liked a spirited woman."

For a moment she looked confused by his boldness. She started to stammer something, then shook her head and looked away. "Mr. Wagner's condition hasn't changed," she said abruptly, as if grasping for something to defuse what she wasn't entirely certain was even lit yet. "He's drooling a little blood, but resting easier."

Rusty figured that after the beating Wagner's already frail body had taken between the wrecked stage and the station, he wasn't likely to last long. He would be basically useless from a defensive standpoint, and so was unimportant as far as Rusty was concerned. He didn't care how the man was resting, but he didn't want to spoil the moment either. Grinning, he said, "Well, you are a hell of a nurse, I'll say that, and I was wondering if you'd take a look at a swelling I seem to be developing."

Ruby's face reddened, and Rusty chuckled. "I figured you knew the lay of the land," he said.

"You've mistaken me for someone else, Mr. Cantrell."

"I don't think so." He edged closer. "You are a fine-looking woman, Ruby, and I've always admired fine-looking women."

The confusion vanished from Ruby's face. She looked at him with sudden scorn. "Save your flattery and your innuendos, Cantrell. They won't work on me. I married a man like you when I was seventeen, caught like a little fly in his web of lies, so I've been down that pike before. I won't fall for it again."

Rusty laughed. "Down the pike, and on it a time or two, I'd wager."

Ruby tried to brush past him, but he grabbed her arm and pulled her back. His voice turned harsh, cutting the deep silence of the room like shards of broken glass. "I've never seen a whore blush before. What would you do for a dollar?"

She spun toward him, her free arm flashing in the dim light. Rusty caught her wrist before her hand could connect with his face. He twisted it cruelly, forcing a cry from her throat. With her back arched awkwardly and her breasts straining against the fabric of her robe, Rusty's desire flamed. He pulled her roughly against him and tried to kiss her. She cried out again, softly yet, and turned her face away. He let go of her arm and brought his hand up to maul her breasts.

"You are something, aren't you?" he breathed hoarsely. "A regular little hellcat in bed, I'll bet."

"Let me go, damn you. Cantrell! I swear I'll scream."

"Go ahead." Rusty laughed. "See if ol' Dawson'll come running to your rescue."

"He'd kill you."

Rusty gave her wrist another savage twist, then pushed her away. He drew his right-hand Colt and shoved the barrel into her throat. The ratcheting of sears as he cocked the revolver sounded loud in the quiet of the night. "Go ahead, whore," he rasped. "Call him."

Fear came into Ruby's eyes at last, and Rusty felt something inside him loosen and fall away. He pulled the Colt back and flashed a grin. "You ain't so tough. Neither is Dawson. You keep that sonofabitch away from me, or I'll blow a hole in his head. Understand?"

Ruby nodded silently, and Rusty's grin flashed menacingly. "See, you could learn. A little time and you wouldn't care who you spread your legs for."

"Leave me alone," Ruby said softly.

"Well, I'll think about it, and let you know what I decide. How's that?"

"Leave . . ." Ruby licked her lips. "Leave the girl alone, too."

"Emma?" Rusty laughed. "Emma and me are gonna get married. We haven't talked about it yet, but ol' Emma's ripe for plucking, and I'll bet she'll say yes."

"You bastard." Ruby's hand flew up to strike him.

Rusty grabbed her wrist with his left hand and sank his right fist into the softness of her stomach. She gasped and croaked and curled around his arm, hanging there with one knee bent upward until Rusty stepped back. She collapsed to the plank floor, gagging, writhing, fighting for air. Rusty's breath came hard, and there was a roaring in his ears. He thought about kicking her, but was afraid that he might go too far. He didn't want to damage her, just to break her.

Boots thumped the floor outside, and young Grady Shaw groaned from his bed, stirring under his blankets. Rusty blinked and straightened from a half crouch. He looked at the Colt in his hand, but couldn't remember pulling it. Almost self-consciously, he dropped it back in its holster. Nudging Ruby's knee with the toe of his boot, he said, "It's late. You'd best get to bed."

Ruby turned toward him. Her face was pale, her eyes socketed in shadows. "My God," she whispered.

Suddenly uneasy, Rusty made a brief motion above her. "Just . . . go to bed. Morning will come early."

He pulled the door open and slipped into the main room. Frank Cassidy stood in the kitchen, his cheeks bulging with meat cut from the remnants of last night's supper. "I ain't never ate buff'ler meat before," Frank managed around a full mouth. "This is pretty damn good."

"You're supposed to be on watch." Rusty put his hand on his Colt so Frank would listen.

Frank's eyes narrowed, shifting between Rusty's hand and face. "Ain't nothing to see. Injuns don't attack at night—everybody knows that."

"Only fools know that for sure. Get back up there and keep your eyes peeled. I'll send Clyde up in an hour or so to relieve you."

Frank didn't move immediately. He was a little slow and not particularly brave, but he had his pride too. After nearly a minute, Frank nodded. Picking up his knife and the slab of meat he'd cut his first slice from, he said, "Sure, Rusty. I'll go keep watch."

Frank took his time even then, and Rusty didn't relax his guard until the man was out of the room and the door shut behind him. He started across the room to retake his seat, but Kane's chuckling stopped him. He spun, his hand flashing once more to the Colt at his waist.

"You 'n me are a lot alike, sonny," the old man spoke from the humped robe beside the front door.

Rusty snorted. "Bullshit."

"Go ahead and laugh, but it's true. We want the same things."

Kane's assertion piqued Rusty's curiosity. Cautiously, he replied, "And what's that, old man?"

"Outta here, boy. Free of these deadbeats hangin' around our necks. And the women. I reckon we both want the women."

Rusty licked his lips. "You're full of shit, old man."

Kane lay back, pulling the robe over his ears. "Naw, sonny. You think about what I said. There's a few things I want, too. Mebbe so we could help one another t' git 'em."

"What did you have in mind?"

"You jus' think about it, sonny. Jus' let it simmer awhile.

Them Cheyenne, they ain't gonna wander off t'morrow the way Dawson says they will. They got 'em something they want, too."

"Are you talking or farting?" Rusty flared. "I'm having a little trouble telling the difference."

Kane laughed softly. "T'morrow night, sonny. You want outta here? You wanna git shut of them others? You want the women? T'morrow night, you be ready. We'll do it, by God. We'll do it."

CHAPTER 10

IN THE EAST the stars were beginning to fade, although it would be some time yet before there was enough light to attack the stone lodge.

Medicine Wolf had not moved throughout the long night. He had watched Sun sink from this place, pulling the light after it. Darkness had mantled the sky and the air cooled and became uncomfortable. Now Sun was chasing the night—the circle complete.

It was good when things came full circle, Medicine Wolf mused. It was the way of Man Above, and of their Mother, the earth. It was the right way, a way that was easy to understand. But Medicine Wolf also knew that within himself there was a circle incomplete, a thing left unfinished. He remembered the conversation he'd had last night with Looks Far Man and Yellow Knife.

It had been late when his two friends approached. The others were camped over the hill, along the Rattlesnake where they had retreated yesterday after the white-eye with the long-shooting gun had driven them away from the coach. They had returned to the wounded despite Medicine Wolf's admonitions that they should remain close to the stone lodge. Yellow Knife had led the dissent, his authority enhanced by his insistence on continuing his fight with the white-eyes despite his broken arm.

Last night Looks Far had hesitated in the darkness, then came forward to face him. His voice had been low, halting. "My brother is wounded."

It was a statement Medicine Wolf hadn't understood at first.

"He feels the pain of his woman's passing to the Other Side," Looks Far went on. "It is like a hole carved into his heart."

Medicine Wolf's anger stirred quickly. "Medicine Wolf is a warrior. I will fill the emptiness of my woman's passing with the blood of the white-eyes."

"The hole inside Medicine Wolf has already been filled," Yellow Knife said angrily. "But not with the blood of your enemies."

Medicine Wolf held himself in. Looks Far Man seemed saddened by Yellow Knife's remark, but not particularly surprised. Looks Far Man said, "White Hawk is like a badger burrowed beneath a great rock. We only waste ourselves trying to dig him out. I think we should ride away, and wait for White Hawk to emerge from his burrow."

"White Hawk is not a badger. A badger is a great fighter that fears nothing. There is honor in a badger's heart. White Hawk is like a Pawnee who has no heart, no courage. Medicine Wolf will not wait for such a creature to grow tired of hiding. I will smoke White Hawk from his burrow."

"Medicine Wolf forgets that stone does not burn," Yellow Knife said icily.

Again, Medicine Wolf held his anger in check. Only the tightness of his voice betrayed the emotion he felt. "Yellow Knife does not think with his mind. Perhaps his thinking has been dulled by the pain in his arm. There are other ways to smoke White Hawk from the stone lodge."

"Ways that cost the lives of friends and brothers! Ways that will cause wailing in the lodges of our women when we return to our village, and empty bellies for our children when Winter returns to lock the plains in ice and drive the buffalo far away!"

"They are warriors' ways!"

"They are foolish ways!" Yellow Knife countered indignantly.

"It is not a thing for one man to decide," Looks Far interrupted. He squatted so that he and Medicine Wolf were equal in height. "Others also say too many have died, my brother, and that too many have been wounded by the rifles of the white-eyes. I think they are right."

His voice barely above a whisper, Medicine Wolf replied, "I am not a god. I cannot command others to do what is not in their hearts. But I will stay. I will not give up until White Hawk is dead."

"Then you stay alone!" Yellow Knife sneered.

"No," Looks Far said quietly, rocking back on his heels and putting his hands on his knees. A smile came to his face, warm with friendship. "I will stay and fight with Medicine Wolf. He is my brother, and my friend."

"If you want to fight, let us find some longknives to kill," Yellow Knife argued. "Let us go pull another iron horse from its tracks to puff in the grass like a dying buffalo. Let us find a fight where there is honor and glory in the battle, instead of breaking our arrows upon stone."

"My friend Yellow Knife is a brave man," Looks Far said in feigned innocence. "You have taken many scalps, and counted coup against the Pawnee, the Osage, and the white-eyes. You would not be considered a woman if you rode away."

Medicine Wolf smiled inwardly at Looks Far's manipulation. Yellow Knife immediately bristled.

"I am not a coward who is afraid to fight the white-eyes," Yellow Knife said. "But even the bravest man cannot fight stone."

"Yellow Knife should go," Looks Far said in a thoughtful tone. "There are plenty of white-eyes to fight along the Smoky Hill River. But I think I will stay. I want to retrieve the bodies of Crazy Boy, Spotted Dog, Cloud Watcher, and Falls In The Water."

Yellow Knife was silent. The four were dead warriors they hadn't been able to bring out of the trees after last evening's attack. Medicine Wolf stared into the darkness where his feet hid, aware of Looks Far's patient waiting, of Yellow Knife's turmoil. Finally, Yellow Knife said, "We should try to steal their horses at least. They will be easy to break out of the corral."

"Yes, they would be easy to steal," Looks Far agreed. "But how will the badger run if we cut off its feet? I think we should rescue the bodies of our brothers, but leave the horses."

"Looks Far is right," Medicine Wolf said. He hadn't considered his friend's philosophy before this, hadn't looked further ahead than his own dismal failure as a war leader. But he saw now that what Looks Far said made sense. They must leave the white-eyes their ponies if they wanted White Hawk to attempt escape.

Yellow Knife made no answer, and after several minutes he turned and walked off. Looks Far remained a while longer, but eventually he also returned to the camp along the creek.

Medicine Wolf had remained, staying awake throughout the night and praying to his spirit helper, the white buffalo wolf. But the white wolf ignored Medicine Wolf's pleading, and now a new day was dawning. It was time to return to camp, to lead his men into fresh battle.

Medicine Wolf knew it was foolish to do this thing. If a man's spirit helper deserted him, he should withdraw as a leader and seek the advice of a medicine man. Perhaps a medicine man would suggest he seek another vision. Perhaps he had offended his relatives on the Other Side by walking over the ground where they had been massacred, and their spirits needed appeasement. There were many things he might have done to offend the spirits; many that might have been offended. Medicine Wolf didn't pretend to have the insight to understand the world of spirits and helpers and taboos. That was why he needed to seek the advice of a holy man, one who understood these things and could help him understand them. Without the blessing of Man Above, without the help of his medicine, he was like a blind man wandering the prairie.

But hatred was a medicine in itself. It curdled in his stomach like the sour milk of a slaughtered buffalo cow. When he thought of White Hawk's treachery, or of Red Willow Woman's corpse lying half frozen in the mud along the Washita, his judgment was clouded by a tunneling fog. When he thought of these things—and there was no time when they were not on his mind—all else faded. In the red mist of his anger, he did not worry that the white wolf hadn't visited him last night, or that he might have offended his relatives on Sand Creek. All that mattered was that he avenge Red Willow Woman's murder.

By killing White Hawk and the others, Medicine Wolf would bring the circle to a close.

In the cool early-morning light, Clint slowly prowled between the station and the stable, eyes cast to the ground. The prints of unshod Indian ponies were clearly evident in the dust and grass. So too were the crusty pools of dried blood where Cheyenne warriors had fallen and died. But the bodies of the four dead Indians DeWeese and Wilson had dragged downwind from the station were gone.

The horses and mules were still penned in the corral.

Wilson was squatted beside the creek where it curved through the corral, his carbine butted to the soft ground. He stood as Clint approached, a puzzled expression scoring his face.

"I don't know," Clint said in response to Wilson's unspoken question.

"Maybe they knew we were out here," Wilson replied, glancing uncertainly toward the mules milling around the mounds of hay DeWeese was forking into the corral. It was obvious he didn't believe his own words. The Cheyenne had returned in the night to recover the bodies of the warriors killed in yesterday's sundown raid, but they hadn't made any attempt on the horses and mules in the corral. It didn't make sense.

"When would something like that stop a Cheyenne from trying?"

Wilson shook his head, staring downcreek. His brows were veed in brooding contemplation. "It's hard to second-guess an Indian," he said hesitantly. "Perhaps they . . ." The words trailed off.

Amos Booth, Kane, Rusty Cantrell, and Shorty Phelps came out of the station. Booth looked pale and weak, and there was a drag in his step, but he'd refused Ruby's suggestion that he remain in bed that morning. He was determined to overcome his exhaustion by sheer perseverance. He carried his arm in a sling, and picked at his teeth with a splinter peeled from the edge of the table. They had eaten in shifts that morning, after the first gray light of dawn had come and gone without an attack.

Booth and Phelps started toward the corrals, but Kane and Cantrell held back, standing close in conversation. Clint's eyes narrowed suspiciously as he watched the two men. Stopping beside Wilson, Booth took the toothpick from his mouth and managed a lopsided grin. "Young Grady just woke up. Ruby's feeding him some broth now. He's a little foggy yet, but talking."

Wilson smiled, the first since they'd arrived. "That's good news, Amos. Grady is a likable young man."

Booth nodded happily. "Grady is a good kid, all right. I would have hated to see him go under."

"Question is, can he handle a gun?" Shorty Phelps said. He stood slightly apart from the others, where he could keep all three men and the station in sight. Distrust was draped across his face like a banner.

The light faded from Booth's eyes. "Grady will fight if

he's capable," he replied stiffly, then deliberately turned his back on the slightly built gunman.

Phelps's head jerked back as if he'd been slapped. His hand rocked toward the butt of the revolver on his right hip. Clint shifted his weight from one foot to the other, swinging around to face Phelps straight on, and Wilson twitched the muzzle of his carbine. But Phelps seemed immune to their implied threat. His gaze never wavered. In a quietly venomous tone, he said, "You ain't enough."

Booth turned back, frowning. "What did you say?"

"I said you three ain't enough." Phelps's voice quavered, and his gaze drilled into Booth. "If you ever turn your back on me again I'll put a bullet in it. I swear to God I will."

Cantrell and Kane had wandered closer, but they stopped short at Phelps's words. Kane looked at Clint with a tight grin stretching the flesh over his cheeks.

Booth's Adam's apple bobbed twice, and his good hand balled into a fist. Phelps had all but challenged him, and it would be a tremendous blow to his pride to back down. Clint glanced at Cantrell, but the curly-haired gang leader seemed content to watch.

"Best let it go, Amos," Wilson said softly. "You have other responsibilities."

Booth's shoulder was hunched and rigid, his face splotchy with anger. For a moment Clint thought he might actually try to take Phelps, wounded shoulder or not, but the moment passed and the driver's face sagged in bitter defeat.

Phelps blinked several times, as if coming out of a trance. He let his hand slide away from his revolver, but his expression didn't change. Spinning on his heels, he stalked toward the stable in jerky, head-popping strides.

Cantrell chuckled, though softly enough that Phelps wasn't likely to hear him. "That was pretty stupid," he told Booth. "Shorty ain't a man you'd want to tangle with."

Shame and indignation mixed equally on Booth's face as he turned to Cantrell. "What are you vultures doing here?" he grated. "Who are you running from?"

"Why, we're running from redskins, same as you." Laughing, Rusty retreated toward the trees behind the house.

"I don't know that I wouldn't rather have the Cheyenne inside and that bunch in the hills," Wilson said somberly.

Kane cackled laughter, sliding back. "You boys have bit off more'n you kin chew, ain't cha? Shoulda listened to ol' Kane, is what you shoulda done. Been halfway to Larned by now, I woulda."

Or Denver, without a backward glance, Clint thought disgustedly. Kane walked away, leaving the trio alone. Almost curiously, Booth said, "He don't look nearly as worried as he did yesterday."

"He's got something up his sleeve," Clint said suddenly, remembering Kane's recent friendliness with Cantrell.

"I'd say he's got his eye on one of the horses," Wilson said. He looked at Clint. "It'd be your dun he'd try to steal. Everything else belongs to Cantrell's bunch, or are L&P mules."

Clint knew Wilson was right. Kane wouldn't steal a mule if there was a horse available. A horse was faster and not nearly as smart as a mule, qualities Kane would look for in an animal. There was Clint's bay packhorse, but it was too small, and only green broke. And he wasn't likely to steal from Cantrell's bunch either; they were too gun-happy, too dangerous.

That left only the dun, and Clint swore softly.

Emma lifted the ash-staved bucket off the table and hauled it outside, using the rear door that opened toward the creek. Her knuckles were white around the prickly rope handle, but the rest of her hands were a bright red from the heat of the water and the harshness of the yellow lye soap they used for body, clothes, and dishes alike. Her hands stung between the fingers, where her skin always chapped worse, and she made a mental note to dig out the neat's-foot oil her father kept for the harness leather so she could tend to them before they cracked and bled. She thrust her lower lip out in a pout, thinking of the greasy feel and the smell of neat's-foot oil on her hands.

Emma hated her hands more than any other part of her body. They seemed big and awkward, roughened by water and wind, calloused by the hickory handle of a garden hoe she'd worn slick over the years. The ugliness of her hands only reflected the dreariness of her life here, and when she dreamed of better places, she imagined having slim, delicate hands, pale as moonlight.

She upended the bucket and tossed the sudsy water away from her, creating a strip of shallow mud that would probably dry in the wind long before the sun cleared the horizon. Setting the bucket down, she turned to face the growing dome of light where the sun was just cresting the hills. Despite the early hour there was already a sheen of sweat glistening on her forehead. She shivered in the morning chill and folded her arms beneath her small breasts.

She longed to go inside and freshen up. She felt dirty and smelly after cleaning away the refuse of a big meal. She wanted to douse her face and arms in lilac water, and run a comb through her hair before the men returned. This morning, she'd tied her hair behind her with her best red ribbon, but that was hardly enough . . . considering.

Spurs chinked in the grass behind her, and she turned and felt her heart sink a little. Of all the people to find her here, to see her in such an untidy mess.

Rusty Cantrell came around the corner of the station and stopped when he saw her. Then he gave her his best smile, like it was a piece of candy he wanted to share, and

Emma's throat constricted suddenly. She wanted to pick up her bucket and just *run*.

Rusty opened his mouth to speak, but before he could say anything Clyde Cooper's voice rang out from the southeast bastion: "Indians! Indians to the east! Grab your guns, boys, here they come!"

Rusty's hands flashed, a pistol appearing in each one so fast Emma couldn't register having seen them drawn. He ran toward her, putting an arm around her waist and propelling her quickly toward the door. "There they are," he said, nodding past her.

Emma glanced over her shoulder. She could just make out a dozen or so warriors, sitting their stocky mustangs perhaps half a mile beyond the edge of the trees. She could barely make them out in the blinding light of the rising sun.

Rusty hurried her inside, then ran past her into the storage room that led to the southeast bastion. "Bar the door," he shouted over his shoulder as he disappeared.

Emma dropped the heavy oak bar in place. Her mother had already climbed onto the butcher block table with a rifle and opened one of the kitchen's gun slots. Emma grabbed her Springfield from the corner beside the door, lifted down the shooting pouch that contained the musket's paper cartridges and caps, and ducked into her room. She climbed onto the dresser that doubled as a platform for the rifle slot above it and leaned into the cool stone wall. She palmed the latch up and pulled the shutter open.

Sunlight streamed into the room, nearly blinding her. The Indians had all but disappeared in the blurring flood of golden light. They were like the hazy forms of a dream that quickly dissipated upon awakening. In spite of her palpitations, Emma found something stimulating in the nebulous picture; the threat of death brought out a passion for life that had been lacking in her earlier existence.

For all their years on the plains, for all of her father's preparations, they had never been attacked before, and she thrilled at the newfound feelings erupting in her.

There was movement behind her, the musical *ching* of spurs. Panicky, she leaned into the wall, blindly facing the rifle slot and the narrow rectangle of prairie beyond, too flustered to look around. The jingle of spurs quieted a moment, then came on. The dresser shook under Emma's feet as someone clambered up beside her. She blinked, took a deep breath, then finally turned and blinked again.

Rusty slid in beside her, flashing a grin that rivaled the light streaking through the rifle slot. She felt his hip against hers, the stiff leather of an empty holster pushing at her side, the slide of his arm over hers. His rough, masculine odor—a combination of horses and leather and gun oil—struck her like an intoxicant, making her feel suddenly light-headed. He leaned close to her in the cavity surrounding the rifle slot, peering onto the prairie as if all he sought was a different perspective. "Are they coming yet?" he asked innocently.

"I . . . uh, no. No, they're . . . they're still sitting out there." Emma felt flustered, not sure whether she should get down and take the room's only other rifle slot, or insist that Rusty take it.

Before she could formulate a decision, Rusty said, "They'll come soon enough." He pulled back, the smile vanished. He stared at her with an intensity that was like a pick being driven into her chest, piercing her heart.

"You are a brave little girl," he murmured, "and I do admire that."

"I . . ." Emma swallowed and blinked. Her voice sounded high-pitched and childish. "I'm not a—a—"

"No," Rusty said gently, his wide blue eyes touching her face. "You aren't, are you? I reckon you're about the prettiest woman I've ever seen, and I've been nearly everywhere. Chicago, St. Louis, Louisville. But you're the prettiest, Emma. Pretty as a flower in spring."

Emma felt weak-kneed and dumb. Words piled up in her throat but couldn't make the climb past her lips. She thought she wanted to die, right there on top of the dresser with a prairie full of Cheyenne braves ready to swoop down on them, and her mother and father in the other room.

So this is how love feels, she thought tremulously.

Then her mother stuck her head in the door, making a little sound of dismay when she spotted the two of them standing so close. Her voice cracked across the room like a driver's oiled whip. *"Emma Jean!"*

Emma jerked away and almost tumbled off the dresser. Rusty grabbed her and pulled her back, wrapping his strong arms around her and crushing her against him before she could react. Emma thought surely she would die then, but her mother's voice brought her back to her senses.

"Get down from there! Right now!"

Rusty was grinning broadly, but he gave her up without struggle. Emma jumped down, her knees giving a little.

"You come out here with me," her mother commanded, speaking to Emma but staring at Rusty.

"Yes, Mama." She started forward.

"And bring your musket," her mother said with disgust. She gave Rusty another hard look, then turned her back on him. Emma followed obediently, the heat of Rusty's stare burning into the back of her neck. And in her chest her heart sang, free at last.

She was in love. She hadn't known it could be this wonderful.

CHAPTER 11

THE CHEYENNE WAITED until the sun climbed above the horizon. Then they feinted, coming as far as the edge of the rambling cottonwood grove before veering to the south and disappearing behind the dusty green foliage without firing a shot.

Clint followed them with the Whitworth, his finger tightening on the trigger when the Cheyenne reached the trees, then easing off as they changed directions.

Kane swore, glaring at Clint. "Somethin' wrong with that trigger finger o' yours, sonny?" he asked.

Clint ignored him, trying to follow the progress of the Cheyenne through the tattered veil of leaves and branches. He worried that they might try to swing around him and come in from another direction, but after nearly half an hour of tense waiting he decided their attack had been only a ploy, a dozen copper-skinned fingernails drawn slowly across a prairie slate.

"Perhaps they didn't care for our morning stroll," Wilson suggested drolly. "Leaving the cell is hardly model behavior for a bunch of inmates like us."

"I coulda got a couple them bastards if they'd a come closer," Kane said loudly. "Coulda picked 'em off clean if I'd a had me a rifle with fancy vernier sights."

Shorty Phelps seemed to perk up at Kane's grousing. He fixed Clint with a gauging stare and said, "That's a Yankee sniper's rifle, ain't it, Dawson?"

Wearily, Clint leaned away from his rifle slot in the south wall. He glanced at Kane for the trouble he'd brought up, let his gaze touch the others scattered around the room, then looked at Phelps. "More or less," he admitted. "I bought it off an immigrant at Fort Kearney, then sent it back to St. Louis to have it converted to a breechloader."

"Were you a Yankee, Dawson?" Phelps asked.

Clint's fingers tightened around the Whitworth.

"Does it make a difference?" Wilson asked, coming forward with his carbine slanted across the crook of his arm, the muzzle pointed almost casually toward Phelps's chest. Pausing in the middle of the room, he said, "The war's over. Let it drop, Phelps."

When Phelps started to bristle, Wilson deliberately cocked the Sharps. "We've got enough problems right now without you dredging up old hatreds. I'm telling you to let it drop."

Cantrell chuckled loudly from the other room.

Phelps drew himself up. His left-hand revolver was still holstered, but he held the other one in his right hand, its barrel pointed toward the floor.

Clint's stomach tightened alarmingly. He knew Phelps could flip it up and snap a shot from waist level in half the time it would take him to swing the Whitworth around. Likely he was fast enough to drop Wilson first, even before Wilson could squeeze the Sharps trigger. Wilson probably knew that as well, but he was a different breed than Booth, who had backed down from Phelps earlier. War had tempered Wilson's personality; he wouldn't be nearly as quick to surrender to doubt or fear. He matched Phelps's stare easily, the Sharps muzzle unwavering.

Rusty Cantrell moseyed into the room, grinning as he scratched his whiskered jaw with the front sight of his Colt. He watched quietly for a moment, then said, "Ol' Wilson and Dawson are the best rifle shots in the bunch, Shorty. Might be best if you didn't kill 'em until we whip these Cheyenne."

"Don't need them," Phelps replied brusquely. "Don't need these bastards one bit."

"Yeah, but if you kill everyone—"

"He's not going to kill anyone," Wilson cut in sharply. "Unless it's a Cheyenne."

Cantrell shook his head with mock sadness. "Now see, Wilson, you just threw a bucket of coal oil on a flame when I was trying to put out the fire."

But Phelps suddenly laughed, his muscles relaxing visibly. Unconsciously, Wilson sighed, his grip loosening around the Sharps.

"Don't worry, Wilson," Phelps said in a lightened tone. "We'll finish this before I ride out." He looked at Cantrell and said, smiling, "This one's got some grit, Rusty. I changed my mind about killing him. Maybe I'll just shoot him."

Cantrell nodded, but his expression didn't change. "Well, that's good, Shorty. Always give a family man a chance, I say."

As the Sharps muzzle dipped toward the floor, Phelps moved, his revolver coming up so fast he'd already fired before Clint could even shout a warning.

The report of the shot was loud in the closed room, deafening. It hammered at Clint's ears and rocked him on his heels. He started to bring the Whitworth up even as Wilson spun toward the floor, but Phelps swung the smoking revolver toward him, stopping the muzzle on a line with Clint's chest. He had his second revolver out, too, cocked and aimed at Booth's stomach. Cantrell had also drawn his second revolver, covering the others in the room. For a long moment, no one moved or spoke. Then Emma Wilson screamed and ran to her father's side, and Polly Wilson fainted.

The seconds ticked past. Rusty could feel the tension stretch to the point of breaking. Emma's frantic sobbing clubbed the air . . . it beat at the rafters and seemed to rattle the pots and pans in the kitchen. Then with a small, startled gasp, her wailing quickly tapered off. Rusty glanced at the girl and saw her father struggling to sit up. The Sharps lay beside him, its lock smashed.

Relief welled up unexpectedly in Rusty, until he saw the way Shorty was staring at Clint Dawson. Shorty hadn't killed Wilson, but his anger was on the loose now. Shorty was going to kill Dawson if someone didn't stop him. Rusty didn't much give a damn about Dawson, but he knew that whatever seed of interest he might have planted in Emma Wilson's head atop the dresser would expire in the face of such unprovoked bloodshed.

Rusty turned his Colts on Shorty, thumbing the hammers back. "Put 'em up, Shorty," he said regretfully, knowing even as he spoke that he had crossed an irreversible line with the gunman, and that one of them would die within the next few minutes.

Clyde, Abe, and Frank had entered the room at the sound of Shorty's shot. They stood in the doorway now, watching the events unfold between Rusty and Shorty with cool aplomb. With a sudden, sickening dawning, Rusty realized Kane was right. There was no brotherhood between them anymore; whatever sense of loyalty had existed in the past had died with a couple of laughing, towheaded kids in Iola. His association with all of them seemed suddenly repugnant; he wished he could turn his Colts on each of them, wiping out the ugliness of what they had done.

He wouldn't, yet the thought of it brought a cocky smile to Rusty's lips. He focused his attention on Shorty. Less than fifteen feet separated them, and he knew neither of them was likely to miss at that distance.

"You always were a chicken-shit little coward," Shorty said.

Rusty pulled the trigger in answer, dodging to the side as Shorty turned his revolver on him. His bullet took Shorty in the chest, slamming him back against the wall.

Shorty's bullet passed through the space where Rusty had stood only a scant second before, plowing into a chest of drawers behind him. A sliver of wood jumped like a tick from the drawers to pierce the flesh of his arm, but Rusty ignored the sting. He fired again, then a third time.

Shorty rocked on his heels, shoulders braced against the stone wall. Slowly, his revolvers sank toward the floor, his fingers relaxing their grip. He swallowed once, his eyes already dulling. Then his feet slid out from under him and he slid limply to the floor. The sharp, pungent odor of urine filled the room, competing with the acrid sting of gunsmoke.

Rusty straightened and swallowed a deep breath, unaware until then that he had even been holding it. He looked at Clyde and the others, but no one spoke, and he could read nothing in their eyes.

Clint cocked his rifle, the sound barely audible above the ringing in Rusty's ears. He glanced at Clint and frowned.

"Holster your guns, Cantrell," Clint ordered.

"I saved your life, Dawson."

"Holster them."

Rusty shrugged and complied. At the door, Frank and Abe shifted uncertainly, neither man aware of Grady Shaw standing behind them with a double-barreled shotgun.

"Shorty was going to kill you, you know?" Rusty said to Clint.

Clint was looking at Emma. "How's your pa?" he asked.

The station manager struggled to his feet. He looked slightly stunned, either from the shock of Shorty's bullet smashing the carbine in his hands, or by the violence of the last couple of minutes. "I'm okay. The little sawed-off runt hit my rifle instead of me."

Rusty laughed at Wilson's cockeyed assumption, and Clyde snorted. "Shorty could castrate a fly with those pistols," Clyde said. "He hit what he aimed for."

"What the hell was eating him?" Booth asked, looking around the room with a perplexed expression. "No one here did anything except take him in and feed him."

"Ol' Shorty was always touchy," Rusty confided. "Sometimes he'd get a burr under his saddle like that and wouldn't rest until he killed someone." He smirked at Clint. "Generally the people he killed needed it, for one reason or another."

"Or if they didn't, I'm sure he could come up with a reason," Wilson replied crossly.

"Yep, he was funny like that," Rusty agreed. "But he isn't going to bother anyone now." His gaze swung back to Clint. "So what are you going to do, Dawson? You can't shoot us all with a single-shot rifle."

Clint let the Whitworth's barrel drop. "Someone had better get back on watch," he announced to the room at large. "Cantrell and I will drag Shorty outside and bury him." Glancing at Wilson, he said, "We'll need some shovels and picks."

Rusty laughed. "Whoa, Dawson. I ain't digging a grave."

"You killed him, you can help bury him," Clint said flatly.

"Like hell. Let the crows have him." He was aware of Emma's horrified look, from the floor beside her father's legs, but figured he could smooth those troubled waters when the time came. He might kill a man to save his image with a woman, but he sure as hell wasn't going to blister his hands on a shovel for it.

"I'll help dig the grave," Wilson said. He turned toward the door and saw his wife crumpled on the floor. He shouted, "Polly!" and darted across the room. Emma scrambled after him, and young Shaw foolishly set his shotgun aside to help.

Almost casually, Rusty lifted a Colt from its holster. He caught Clint's sharp, suspicious glance, but only grinned.

For a moment he had lost control of the situation, but he had it back now. He wouldn't lose it again.

Rusty walked past Abe and went into the main room. He spotted Kane's ivory mane to one side and motioned with a shift of his head for the old man to follow him. "Come on, Kane," he said, angling toward the northwest bastion. "Let's you'n me keep watch together a while. We've got some palavering to do."

Rusty carefully rolled and lit a cigarette, holding the lucifer up afterward to admire the steadiness of his hand. His physical control, no matter what the situation, was a thing he took pride in, and he wanted Kane to notice it now.

He sat cross-legged on the small wooden platform of the bastion, his right knee propped against the stone wall, the left slanted above the old frontiersman's skinny leg. It was cramped atop the platform, but private. They could talk quietly and not have to worry about anyone from below overhearing what they said.

Rusty had a growing interest in Kane's guarded promises of the night before. The old blowhard had been right about one thing: Rusty wanted to get shut of his gang. It was time to move on, new territories . . . new partners.

Rusty tipped his hat back and studied the old man curiously. Kane was peering nervously through one rifle slot, then another. When he'd examined each view carefully, he sank back with a heavy, unconscious sigh. "Horses is still there," he announced. "Man has to keep an eye on his ponies ever' second if he don't want some Injun stealin' 'em."

"You an expert on redskins, Kane?"

Kane glanced at him suspiciously. "Mayhaps I know me a bit. Been out here a good long time."

"You're wearing Indian clothing," Rusty observed.

"Lotsa folks wear Injun clothing," Kane replied defensively. "Mocs and such. Don't mean nothin'."

"No, I didn't say it did. I just wondered if you knew your way around the plains. We cut our pins tonight, we're going to have to do some fancy riding. Do you know which way to go?"

The old man's face took on a sudden light, and he leaned forward eagerly, breathing the sour taste of bad teeth into Rusty's face. "Damn right I do, sonny. West is the direction we want, only south first. Pick up the Santy Fe Trail and find us a caravan of traders to ride with till we get shut of Cheyenne and 'Rapaho country. Then north t' Idaho. They got 'em a new strike up there."

"In Idaho? I haven't heard anything about it."

"Not many has yet. Feller back t' Independence told me so. I wouldn't a risked comin' back acrost these plains this time of year if I didn't think it was so. Too late to catch me a steamer up the Missouri River, and if what I heared was true, they'll be a passel of folks cramming upriver come spring. I am t' beat 'em to it." He leaned back and wiped at his lips. "Came the southern route 'cause I'd heard about the Cheyenne trouble along the Smoky Hill Trail and on the Platte. Figured t' dodge 'em thisaway."

Rusty laughed. "Shitty luck, old man."

"Whadda you mean by that?" Kane bristled.

Rusty studied the old man thoughtfully. He knew Kane wasn't telling him everything. The question was, how much was he leaving out, and how important was it?

"She's a pretty little thing, ain't she?" Kane said then, changing the subject. "That station manager's daughter. Ripe as a red cherry, she is."

"Little young for you, old-timer."

"Ain't me that wants her," Kane answered shrewdly, watching Rusty's face closely. "It's you what wants her, sonny. Saw it yesterday, I did. You got the wants bad. She's like a new rifle. Like this here Henry." He lifted the brass-framed repeater. "Saw 'er in a gun-shop window in Independence, I did, and took a shine to 'er right off. Only thing is, they wanted a hundred dollars for 'er, and that's a heap of money in any man's poke. Heap of money."

"I notice you managed somehow."

Kane chuckled coarsely. "Yep, I did. Plucked 'er like a pea off'n a vine. That's what you gotta do, sonny. You gotta just grab what you want. Me, I want the other one, that Ruby woman, but you kin have the kid."

The old man's confession surprised Rusty. "Ruby?"

Kane's head bobbed. "She is Clint Dawson's woman. Oh, he don't know it yet, and she ain't so sure herownself, but I seed it. Seed it plain, I did. That's why I want her. Jus' for a while. Jus' long enough."

"Do you hate Dawson that much?"

"Don't hate Dawson, rightly. Jus' wanna make 'im see he ain't so smart. I want outta here, too, and sometimes a white woman is a good thing t' have, case we get cornered by a bunch of hungry redskin bucks somewheres. No guarantee, but it's always good t' have a little something t' trade."

Rusty shut his eyes, shaking his head. "No. I'm not a slaver or a rapist. I won't give a woman to Indians to use like some whore."

"Sure you will," Kane replied, chuckling. "You'n me, we're alike, sonny. You jus' ain't seen all the potential yet."

"No."

"Yeah, you is. I done seed it, boy. T'night we're gonna grab the women and the horses, and we're gonna ride outta here. You can do what you want with your little girl, but you'll bring 'er along. I'd wager my Henry on that."

Rusty opened his eyes, staring at the curved stone wall across from him. Kane was right, he realized with a little start of shame. They were quite a bit alike, after all.

CHAPTER 12

THE CHEYENNE MADE their first real attack on the station around midmorning. Clint had been sitting at the kitchen table with a cup of coffee, letting the muscles in his shoulders relax while the sweat of carving a shallow grave out of hardpan dried to a dark stain on his shirt. They'd buried Shorty Phelps without ceremony, and only Clyde Cooper came out to pay his respects . . . and to rifle through the dead man's pockets.

Wilson sat across from Clint, slowly twirling a white enameled cup between his hands. He stared at the table, his brows arched downward as if in pain. After several minutes of silence, he began to speak quietly, his voice low enough that only Clint heard his words.

"I came out here to find some kind of peace, to get away from so-called civilization. If that sounds a little like a noble fantasy, I guess I'd have to agree right now. But it was a sincere effort at the time."

He stopped, gave the cup another spin, then went on. "I taught theology at Harvard for a while, but basically hated it. I almost cheered when war broke out. I enlisted because I wanted a chance to fight." His voice softened to a whisper. "I already mentioned that I was with Meade, at Gettysburg, when General Pickett's men charged Cemetery Ridge. Lord help me, the men we killed that day . . ."

Watching him, Clint began to grasp the depth of the pain reflected in the station manager's features. Growing up on the frontier, Clint had killed his share of men, white and Indian. But he'd avoided the war. It had seemed too distant, the issues too foreign to a man who'd never been east of the Mississippi.

But he'd heard tales enough to comprehend—even dividing most of what he'd heard by half—the utter devastation of the conflict. Not just in the lives that were lost and property that was destroyed, but in the nation's spirit, too. When he began to view the shattered and disenchanted veterans infiltrating the plains afterward, he'd begun to wonder if he hadn't made a mistake in dividing what he'd heard by half.

"So many dead," Wilson muttered so softly Clint had to lean forward to hear. "Scattered across the fields. Bodies missing limbs. Heads sitting alone like spent cannon balls. And so many. Not just a few, but hundreds . . . thousands. And the expressions on their faces. That was the worse part. Walking over the fields after Lee's retreat, staring at all the dead, seeing what they felt on the moment of death—the terror, the absolute terror. There was no glory in that war, nothing to be gained, or even salvaged."

"Some might say preservation of the nation," Clint supplied gently. "Or the freedom of the slaves."

Wilson snorted cynically. "I haven't seen much evidence of freedom in Reconstruction."

Clint shrugged, feeling too insulated to argue the point with someone who had been there.

"I'd read Tanner, Catlin, and Irving, and I had a vision of the noble redman who lived his life for honor. So after the war I came out here and started this station. I got a contract with the L&P through some military connections and decided to settle down in harmony with my family. I could hunt a little, or trade with the Indians on the side. But I discovered that I was wrong about that, too. The Indians I've met don't resemble nobility at all. They're just people, good and bad, who've been pushed too far the last few years and are now starting to push back.

"I can appreciate their feelings from that perspective.

But as far as my own position, I never got along with them that well. I found their manners arrogant and irritating. I could tolerate them, but I've never felt any sympathy toward them.

"I came out here seeking utopia. Within six weeks the Indians killed and ate my little girl's dog. To me, the Cheyenne are no more noble than the generals who sent their men to be mowed down by the hundreds of thousands by grape and musket balls, or the carpetbaggers who are looting the South even now."

"So where does that put you?" Clint asked with genuine curiosity.

"Disillusioned. But not defeated, my friend. That's why I've stayed, despite the growing hostilities. I wouldn't know where to go that would be less dangerous." Wilson, toying with his cup, seemed on the verge of saying more when a rifle shot from the northwest bastion interrupted his thoughts. On the echo of the rifle's report, Kane shouted, "Here they come! Here they come!"

The Whitworth was leaning against the wall, the shoulder strap of the bullet pouch draped over the muzzle. Clint grabbed the rifle and pouch as he arose, and leapt atop the platform hinged to the west wall of the kitchen. He slid the pouch over his shoulder and knocked the shutter open with the butt of his rifle.

The Indians were coming through the trees like a gust of March wind, riding low over the necks of their ponies and already well advanced when Kane fired. It wasn't until the crack of his rifle that they started yipping and shouting their war cries.

Clint shouldered the Whitworth. The Cheyenne were still a couple of hundred yards away, dodging sinuously through the trees. He caught a brave in his sights and squeezed the trigger just as the Indian swerved his pony; knowing he'd missed, he swore into the billowing powder smoke that obliterated his view.

Kane began a steady fire that did more damage to the sky and trees than to the Cheyenne. His voice shrilled down from the bastion, mindless curses laced with terror. Wilson's carbine boomed from down the wall. Clint lowered the Whitworth's breech and quickly reloaded. The Cheyenne were streaking through the trees, flashing in and out of the shafts of sunlight that slanted like toppling columns to the floor of the grove. Their war cries grew keener as they drew closer, as if they were trying to tear down the thick stone walls with the power of their voices.

Clint pushed the Whitworth's muzzle through the rifle slot, but held his fire. The Cheyenne had spread out as the gunfire from the station increased, but he could see a knot of warriors near the center of the party, riding as if on a mission.

"Look sharp," he called to the others.

"I see 'em," Booth answered tersely. He stood at the kitchen's south wall, his big revolver held ready. Lamplight glinted off his pale, sweating bald head, and he leaned weakly against the stone.

Ruby and Polly had probed for the arrowhead still embedded in Booth's shoulder the night before, but had been forced to give up. It was buried too deep, and they were afraid they might cause permanent damage if they forced it.

"The man needs a real doctor," Polly Wilson had announced in her loud, sterile voice, her mouth drawn into a scowl that seemed to anticipate challenge. But no one challenged her, and Lester DeWeese had added, "Shucks, lotsa men have lived with arrows in their bodies."

But the arrow was taking its toll on the driver's strength. He had spent most of the morning dozing awkwardly in a heavy rocker beside the cold fireplace, cheeks and fingers twitching in pain.

Gunfire blossomed from Cheyenne rifles and pistols. Lead splattered impotently against the walls, and flint-tipped arrows ricocheted off stone with futile *pings*. The whites returned a deadly swath of fire. The repercussions of their weapons created a deafening thunder inside the closed rooms, setting off little blasts of air that brushed Clint's cheeks and stirred his hair.

Most of the warriors came on in a serpentine track, splitting to flow past both side of the station only at the last minute. Clint thumbed the Whitworth's hammer back to full cock, ignoring the angry whine of lead and flint. The knot of four or five Cheyenne who had ridden in on a more or less direct course drew their mounts to a sliding stop beside the main corral, and a brave with a crippled arm leapt off his pony and dashed toward the stables.

Clint dropped him as he crawled between the rails, the Whitworth's slug slamming him through to land sprawling in the churned white dust. Booth peppered the air around a second warrior who was attempting to hack through the chain securing the gate. His third shot opened a long gash across the Indian's ribs that immediately welled blood. The Indian jumped and yelped, dropping his tomahawk.

The Cheyenne gave up then. The bulk of the war party raced past and those within the station turned their weapons on them. The brave who had tried to breach the gate flopped aboard his pony and the whole group raced back the way they had come.

"Clint!"

Ruby's voice sounded muffled through the ringing in Clint's ears, but the panic in her tone was obvious. He jumped down and rushed into the back room, where Ruby, Grady, and young Jack Wilson stood at their posts. Ruby was peering anxiously through a slot, but looked around when Clint entered.

"Something's wrong in the southeast bastion," she told him. "The Indians are trying to get onto the roof, and whoever's up there isn't stopping them."

Clint spun back without answer and ran for the storage

room that led to the bastion where Abe Aaron was stationed. Cantrell, overhearing Ruby's announcement, was also sprinting for the storage room. They met at the door and shouldered through together, cursing each other for getting in the way. Cantrell caught his toe on a sack of grain just inside the door and stumbled, leaving the way clear for Clint, who ducked through the low door into the bastion and stopped. Above him a dark, gnarled hand hung motionless over the edge of the platform. Sunlight shining through one of the slots glistened off a smear of blood across Aaron's knuckles.

Leaning the Whitworth against the wall, Clint started up the ladder. He could hear the Cheyenne outside, shouting excitedly as they attempted to gain the roof. He drew his Colt as he poked his head over the top of the platform. Aaron lay in a heap, his eyes open but glazed in death. There was some blood on his face, a little pool of it gathered around his cheek.

Rusty Cantrell scrambled up the ladder behind him. "Come on, Dawson! Get on up or get out of the way!"

Copper fingers probed inside one of the rifle slots, searching for a solid grip. The Indian must have been standing on the back of his horse. Even that must have been a stretch, Clint thought. Cantrell grabbed Aaron's hand and tried to pull the body out of their way, but he lacked enough leverage to move it. Clint grabbed Aaron's belt and tugged. The Indian had found a grip, a slight bulge in one of the stones, and was pulling himself higher. Desperately, Clint jerked Aaron forward. Cantrell pulled downward on his arm. The lifeless body slid over the edge of the platform like molasses, picking up momentum as the balance of weight shifted.

Clint winced at the sound of the body hitting the floor, but there wasn't time to waste on regret. He clambered onto the platform just as the Indian outside the rifle slot pulled himself up far enough to peer inside. Clint jammed the muzzle of his Colt into the Indian's face and fired pointblank before the Cheyenne could pull away.

His bullet catapulted the Indian away from the bastion. Leaning close to the wall, Clint fired down at the mounted warriors. One of his bullets struck a warrior in the thigh; another creased a neck. Before he could target a third man the Indians whipped their ponies away from the shelter of the bastion, howling their rage.

"Damn," Cantrell exclaimed, falling before one of the slots. "You should've saved a couple for me."

"You'll get your chance," Clint replied, watching the Indians race out of range. A few ineffectual shots from below hurried them on their way.

Cantrell laughed as he leaned back. "Oh, that's okay. I don't mind if you hog the glory."

Clint slid down the wall until he was sitting with his elbows resting across his knees, the Colt hanging limply from his hand. The firing died off below, and a deep, brooding silence began to seep into the station.

"Just enough to keep it interesting, huh?" Cantrell said, meaning the attack.

"Just enough," Clint agreed wearily. He regarded Rusty quietly, remembering the closeness of his and Kane's conversation by the corral that morning, and later in the bastion.

Clint had met a lot of men like Cantrell over the years—hard-shelled drifters with chips on their shoulders. But there was something different about Cantrell. It was a subtle thing, hard to put a finger on, but Ruby had seen it right off, and maybe Wilson had, too. Clint hadn't noticed it until that morning, when Cantrell killed Shorty Phelps. It wasn't the stone-heartedness of the shooting that affected Clint, but the tidiness of it. For Cantrell, killing Phelps had been like shooing away a bothersome gnat, and no more distressing.

Cantrell fished the makings from a vest pocket and

began to roll a cigarette. He looked at Clint and smirked as he put away his tobacco without offering any. "Something eating at you, Dawson?"

"Just wondering," Clint returned easily.

"Well, you don't want to make a habit out of that. I hear it's constipating." He chuckled at his own humor, the smirk never leaving his face.

"You and Kane seem to get along pretty well," Clint said quietly.

Cantrell smoothed the finished cigarette carefully, the smirk winging into a smile. "Ol' Kane doesn't care for you, Dawson. Thinks you're an Indian lover." He glanced thoughtfully at Clint. "Maybe he's right, huh?"

"Kane and I didn't hit it off," Clint acknowledged. "Not that I've lost much sleep over it. But I don't trust Kane, and I don't trust his friends either. You might think on that."

Cantrell's smile never wavered. He dug a match from his pocket and scraped it against the wall. A blue flame burst forth, momentarily distracting Clint's attention. Cantrell let the match drop without lighting his cigarette, and palmed his revolver even as it fell. He laughed at Clint's startled expression.

"You push too much, Dawson," Cantrell said easily. "One of these days it's going to get you killed."

The heat rose in Clint's face; he fought to keep it from his voice. "You're awful fast to pull that damn hogleg, Cantrell. Man like you must have an interesting past."

"There's some who would agree. Maybe if you learn to mind your own business you'll live to hear about it. Maybe. Now me, I ain't got a damn thing against you other than you seem to think mighty high of yourself. But Kane now, he's a different matter. Kane don't care for you at all. I think he'd just as soon see you dead, although I ain't entirely sure why."

"Kane wouldn't be the first man who tried to kill me," Clint replied flatly.

Cantrell cocked his revolver, laughing softly. "Oh, you ain't so tough, Dawson. As a matter of fact, you've turned out to be one of the easiest men to get the drop on I ever saw."

Clint held his tongue, swallowing back the anger that rose in him like bile. He realized he'd underestimated the threat Cantrell and his bunch posed to the others in the station. Wilson's words at the corral that morning came back to him: *I don't know that I wouldn't rather have the Cheyenne inside and that bunch in the hills.*

Clint was still holding his Colt limply in his hand, muzzle pointed to the floor. He said, "I'm going to put my Colt away now."

"Just be easy about it."

Slowly, Clint holstered the revolver. He nodded toward the ladder, then crawled to it, careful not to make any sudden or unexpected moves. Cantrell's Colt followed him all the way. Pausing with his boot on a lower rung, Clint said, "Are you going to bury Aaron, or is that up to us too?"

The smile left Cantrell's face at last, and his voice turned harsh. "That's up to you, Dawson. Bury him, or drag him out on the prairie to rot. It means nothing to me."

CHAPTER 13

IF EMMA THOUGHT she was in love that morning, she wasn't nearly as convinced by the noon meal.

She spooned stewed turnips and buffalo meat into a wooden bowl, leaning back from the kettle to escape the rising cloud of steam that scalded her face and kinked her hair into lifeless whorls that clung damply to her temples. There was a sharp, lancing pain between her shoulder blades that was the result of tension as much as work, although with fourteen to feed (and that not counting Mr. Wagner, who'd come to that morning, or Grady, who'd stumbled back to bed after the Cheyenne attack that morning), there was plenty of work.

Emma wanted to complain to her mother, but between catching Emma and Rusty in the next thing to an embrace on top of the dresser that morning, then fainting dead away when she thought Papa had been shot, her mother wasn't in an approachable mood.

Maybe it was just as well, Emma thought, stealing a glance at Rusty Cantrell. Rusty was sitting on a stool in the main room, cleaning one of his pistols, but each time Emma looked she found his eyes on her, melting straight through her like hot coals through tallow. Her knees got a little weaker every time she thought of him, and that sure wasn't something she was ready to approach her mother about.

She'd thought about approaching Ruby, but there was something about her attitude toward Rusty that held Emma back. At first Emma had feared Ruby wanted him for herself, and she'd been half out of her wits with worry, knowing a simple country girl like herself wouldn't stand a chance against someone as worldly as Ruby Jennings. But then she'd seen that what Ruby felt toward Rusty was just the opposite of what she felt, a revelation Emma wasn't ready to delve into just then.

She fixed up a second bowl of turnips and meat, then, tucking spoons and a towel under her arm, she took it all into the bedroom, avoiding Rusty's eyes as she crossed the main room.

Grady was sitting up in bed in one of her father's clean shirts. The coarse cloth must have irritated the stab wounds that spotted his chest and shoulders, but he had refused to go bare-chested in a house where women could see him. It was sweet in a way, she decided, his caring so much, but it seemed kind of dumb, too. She couldn't help wondering what Rusty would do in the same situation. Somehow, she couldn't picture him yielding to the murmur of modesty, or much else for that matter. The thought brought a flash of irritation at Grady's predictability, his stolid, mule-headed propriety.

Grady noticed her displeasure, and an expression of concern crossed his face. It cooled her irritation to know he watched, and maybe cared.

Wagner was sleeping, propped up on a folded buffalo robe. He seemed to rest easier in an upright position, but his breathing was still shallow and rattly, and there was a scab of dried blood at the corner of his mouth.

Electing not to awaken him, Emma took the food to a dresser, then brought the largest helping to Grady's side. She sat on a chair beside the bed and whispered, "Do you feel up to feeding yourself? I can help if you're—"

"I can do it," Grady answered curtly, seemingly embarrassed by her offer. He hitched himself a little higher, and Emma gave him the bowl and a spoon.

"I'll keep the towel handy," she teased. "Just in case you spill some down your chin."

Grady huffed, but didn't reply. Emma delighted in his embarrassment, but decided against pushing it further. Grady had always been kind to her. She didn't know what it was about him that made her want to torment him.

She looked at Wagner and felt a moment of sadness for the loss she sensed there. It bothered her, seeing the tragedy that sometimes passed through the station—people traveling because of death, people dying. Orphans were the worst, she thought. They pulled at something inside her and twisted it into a knot so tight she sometimes wanted to cry. Tragedy was a part of what made her want to leave.

Grady slurped loudly, breaking her train of thought. She looked at him, then quickly away, pretending not to notice the little trail of broth across his chin that he was hurriedly wiping away with the heel of his hand. But the image stayed with her and made her smile.

"You don't have to look so smug," he accused.

"Hush," she whispered. "You'll awaken Mr. Wagner. If your table manners don't."

Chagrined, Grady dug into his stew—more quietly this time.

"Which do you like best, Grady?" Emma asked suddenly. "Pueblo or Leavenworth?"

"You ask me that question every time I come through here. I ain't changed my mind."

"I think I'd prefer Leavenworth. It sounds bigger and grander."

"You ain't seen much of the world if you think Leavenworth is grand," Grady snorted, scooping up another spoonful.

Emma bit her lower lip. "Grady Shaw, you are just so stupid. I swear I don't know why Amos allows you on his coach. He could kick you off anytime, you know. You're only a shotgun."

As if sensing his advantage, Grady smiled past bulging

cheeks and managed, "Me'n Amos get along. We talk about grand places."

Emma turned away, so furious she wanted to stomp her foot. "I think the only grand place you've ever been is an L&P stable yard!" she told him.

Grady scowled. "That ain't true, Emma. This is a grand place. I like it here." His face reddened, and his voice got a funny hitch as he finished his sentence.

"Now that *is* the stupidest thing I ever heard. If you'd rather be here than Pueblo or Leavenworth, you don't have much ambition."

"Awww," Grady shook his head, staring at the mess of turnips and meat in his bowl. "It ain't the station, Emma. You—you just don't understand."

"Well, I most certainly don't. How could anyone think of Cottonwood Station as being anything but the back door to hell?"

"Your ma catches you using that kind of language, she'd tan your backside good."

"Bet she wouldn't," Emma countered, yet knowing all along that Grady was right. But she wanted to make him see she wasn't a child anymore, that she was a woman now and free to talk like one.

"Bet she would," Grady said, but Emma let it drop. Grady's response sounded immature, and she felt a moment of embarrassment for him. She couldn't imagine Rusty bandying foolishness back and forth so.

Grady finished his stew in silence. When he was done Emma poured him a glass of water from a pitcher on the washstand. Grady drained it and asked for a second glass. "I get mighty dry," he explained.

"Well, my gosh, yes, you do. You've been wounded."

"Well, you took good care of me, Emma. I appreciate that."

Actually, it was her mother and Ruby who'd taken care of him. This was the first time Emma had been in the room since she turned the blankets back yesterday afternoon when her father and Clint Dawson brought him in. But she didn't tell Grady that.

Emma poured another glass of water and set it on the chair beside the bed, within easy reach. Gathering up the dirty utensils, she said, "You'd best rest. Someone will wake you if the Cheyenne come back."

She left the room, pulling the door shut behind her, and when she looked up her eyes went straight to Rusty, as if of their own accord. She stopped, surprised. Rusty smiled and winked, and Emma felt a tightening in her throat, a fresh pounding in her heart. Averting her eyes, she hurried toward the kitchen, more confused now than ever.

Deep in his heart, Medicine Wolf knew that Looks Far was right. They would never root the white-eyes from the stone lodge, not even if they had the big guns of the longknives that rode on wheels. To continue this quest, to watch his friends die in futile charges against the station, was a fanatic's dream.

Yet he could not quit. Neither could he bear waiting for the traitor, White Hawk, to flee. A warrior's blood ran hot, it demanded action. To sit like old women warming their bones under the critical eye of Sun might cool the simmering need for revenge, destroying whatever medicine each man had made before leaving on this raid.

Medicine Wolf knew he could not allow that to happen. He would rather be called a fanatic than have his warriors ride off in disgust, allowing White Hawk's escape. Yet the decision and its probable consequences brought an anguish to Medicine Wolf's breast that challenged even the pain of Red Willow Woman's death.

He had been a respected warrior in the past, had led successful hunting and trading parties over a vast expanse of hostile plains. His peers, and even some of the older warriors, had begun to look to him for advice in matters of the hunt and war. It was only natural that when word arrived from the agency headquarters at Fort Cobb that White Hawk would try to cross the Cheyenne land hidden inside a white-eyes' coach, Medicine Wolf would lead one of the war parties sent out to intercept him.

It was Blue Man Limping who had summoned Medicine Wolf. Medicine Wolf had responded immediately. He found the old chief sitting on the bank of a stream, fletching an arrow with infinite patience. Medicine Wolf's thoughts had been dark even then, but Blue Man Limping's words brought a sudden elation to his heart.

Blue Man Limping approached the subject in the proper manner. He spoke of the weather and the grass, and how the ponies were growing fat. He mentioned the success of the spring hunt, and the importance of the fall hunt yet to come, and brought up the pregnancy of Looks Far's second wife, Swan. Then he tossed a frayed piece of sinew into the stream and watched in silence as the current took it away. When it disappeared, he said, "A hair-face has just returned from the white man's village called Independence. He says that the traitor, White Hawk, whom the white-eyes call Kane, will cross the land of the People on his way to the land of the Ute."

Medicine Wolf's rage churned with the suddenness of a prairie storm, but he held himself in check. "It does not surprise Medicine Wolf that White Hawk will go to the land of the enemies of the People," he said calmly. "White Hawk's heart has turned bad, like meat that has been left too long in Sun's sight."

Blue Man Limping sighed. "It is true that White Hawk's heart is bad, but I am confused by what caused it to rot."

"The badness was always there," Medicine Wolf replied sagely. "It is why White Hawk never accompanied the younger men on the warpath against the Ute or the Pawnee or the Osage. It is why he changed wives, and always coveted what others had. White Hawk's heart is bad. It has always been so."

"Perhaps you are right. It is a sad thing, but there are many sad things that I do not understand."

Tentatively, Medicine Wolf ventured, "White Hawk must be stopped. He must pay for leading the longknives to our village."

"White Hawk led the longknives to Black Kettle's village, which was not his own."

"It was a village of the People," Medicine Wolf retorted, unable to mask his anger any longer. "The blood that stained the ground that day was the blood of the People. White Hawk must pay for this."

"I agree. But the hair-face who brought word of White Hawk's plan did not know when White Hawk would make his journey. He did not know if White Hawk would follow the Platte or the Smoky Hill or the Arkansas. It will take many war parties if he is to be found."

"I will lead a party," Medicine Wolf blurted. He was silent then, waiting for Blue Man Limping's response. Medicine Wolf was young, and he had never led a war party before. He didn't need the permission of the elders to do so now, but he might need their approval in order to convince others to follow him.

Blue Man Limping seemed to ponder Medicine Wolf's proposal for several minutes. It was only afterward that Medicine Wolf realized that Blue Man Limping had already come to this decision. It was why he had summoned Medicine Wolf in the first place.

"You have fought well against the Pawnees," Blue Man Limping said contemplatively. "And you helped Yellow Knife and Cuts His Hair steal many ponies from the Mexicans last summer. You have kept your head in battle. That is good. I think if I were a young brave again, and looking for someone to lead me on a raid against the white-eyes, I would ride with Medicine Wolf."

Pride filled Medicine Wolf's chest and made him sit straighter. He nodded soberly. "I will talk with Looks Far Man and Yellow Knife and Lost His Horse, and ask them to ride with me on the trail to kill White Hawk."

"It is wise that you go to your friends and see if they will follow you. But I think it is also wise to consult the elders who have done this thing many times before. Bear Gut and Broken Tail have both fought the white man's coach. They have been to the land where the white-eyes are thick as leaves on the trees, and they understand the ways of this tribe better than I do. I think you should talk to them, because this time we do not fight the longknives or steal their horses or women. This time we want the man called White Hawk, and that will not be as easy to do."

Medicine Wolf's eyes narrowed; his vision hazed in anger. He wanted to say, *We will stop all the white-eyes that come into the land of the People and kill them. White Hawk will be among them.* Logic stayed his tongue. He knew they could not kill all the white-eyes without bringing the pony-soldiers down on them again. Blue Man Limping was right. They would have to be careful and strike their target before the longknives could organize against them.

"I will talk to Bear Gut and Broken Tail, and seek their advice," Medicine Wolf agreed. "They have fought the whites and Mexicans for twice as long as I have walked the prairies, and their wisdom will help guide me."

Blue Man Limping nodded approvingly, but said no more. Medicine Wolf approached Looks Far and Lost His Horse that afternoon, and by evening a score of younger men clamored to ride with him. But somehow, Medicine Wolf never found time to visit Bear Gut or Broken Tail. He did not seek their advice or pray to the white wolf that was his own spirit helper, and as he rode out of camp at a proud gallop with nearly two score of warriors screaming their victory chants behind him, Medicine Wolf had not been able to look at the lodge of Blue Man Limping. He was afraid the old warrior might be watching.

A warm breeze rustled the leaves overhead, breaking into Medicine Wolf's reverie. He glanced across the broad flat to where the overturned coach lay like a dead beetle, a tiny speck of color in the distance. Involuntarily, his gaze traveled up the windswept ridge behind it to the little rocky knob where the man with the long-shooting gun had snatched victory from Medicine Wolf's grasp. Only a day ago, Medicine Wolf mused. It seemed more like a moon.

Looks Far came over, flopping in the grass beside him. "My brother spends much time inside his mind today," Looks Far observed in a disarmingly absent manner.

"It is a good time to think."

Looks Far glanced at him questioningly, a trace of worry reflected in his dark eyes.

Medicine Wolf hesitated, torn between his hatred for White Hawk and the white-eyes holed up inside the stone lodge, and his friendship for Looks Far Man and the others. But in the end he lowered his head, seeing no other way before him.

"At first I thought Man Above was angry," Medicine Wolf began slowly. "Why else would he bring the man with the long-shooting gun? Why would he allow the white-eyes to escape our traps and reach the stone lodge that not even the wind can destroy? But then my spirit helper came to me." He paused, allowing this lie to sink in, and glanced furtively at his friend.

"What did the white wolf say?" Looks Far asked quietly.

Breathing a shallow sigh of relief, Medicine Wolf went on, "The white wolf told me that the man with the far-shooting gun was an evil spirit, brought from the dark side to test the will of the People. He said that if the People are to survive and keep their land and their buffalo, they must prove their worthiness by killing White Hawk." Slyly,

Medicine Wolf added, "What do you think of this visit, my friend?"

Even if he had doubts, Looks Far was trapped by Medicine Wolf's question. He could not tell a man to ignore the visit of his spirit helper. He could as easily tell him to cut off both arms with his own hands.

But Looks Far was no fool, either. He was a quiet, steady man, without flash, and without the impetuous nature that bred followers. Carefully, Looks Far answered, "If the white buffalo wolf said this thing, it must be true." He paused, stirring the tall grass in front of him with his fingers. "I myself have sought help," he said then. "But the sparrow that sees far has given me a different message. It came to me in a dream last night, and it had tears in its eyes for those who have died attacking the stone lodge. Then it flew over a hill to the south, toward the Ne Shusta, and when I went to follow it I saw the white-haired traitor being dragged away by Cheyenne warriors. Our ropes were around him, and he was screaming in fear like a white woman."

An invisible fist reached into Medicine Wolf's chest and squeezed his heart. He closed his eyes in shame, recognizing the truth in Looks Far's vision and knowing then that Looks Far had recognized the lie in his own.

"My heart is sad," Looks Far said quietly, staring across the broad flat. "When we rode away with White Hawk on our ropes, I did not see you among us."

Medicine Wolf swallowed. "It will be as Man Above decides."

Looks Far nodded. He had already known this. After a couple of minutes he pulled a stem of grass and began to peel it carefully to its core.

The warmth of the breeze felt good on Medicine Wolf's bare shoulders. He concentrated on the touch of the wind and the play of leaf shadows on the tawny grass. In this way he was able to bury the remorse he felt for his lie. The grumblings of several young men rose from the fire, where they waited for slabs of antelope meat to cook. Medicine Wolf chose to ignore the frustration in their voices just as he had chosen to ignore his guilt.

"They are angry," Looks Far remarked. "Yellow Knife was well liked."

"Yellow Knife angered Man Above when he tried to steal the ponies and mules. Those are for White Hawk, so that we may catch him when he flees."

Looks Far gave him an amused glance. "Perhaps you should tell the others of your conversation with your spirit helper. Then they would understand."

Medicine Wolf ignored the implied sarcasm. He knew Looks Far still supported his leadership, even if he didn't believe his vision. They had been friends for a long time.

"They would lose their anger, and after a while they would wander off in search of easier prey," Medicine Wolf explained.

"Ahhh," Looks Far breathed in understanding. "My brother does not think the others would stay if he asked them to?"

"Yellow Knife would have left before Sun dropped into the land of the Utes if the long-shooting gun had not killed him."

"Maybe," Looks Far acknowledged. "But Yellow Knife was one man."

Medicine Wolf shook his head. "It is not right that we talk of the dead. It is not respectful."

"Is it worth the deaths of so many to keep the hatred alive?"

"It is worth whatever must be sacrificed," Medicine Wolf answered bluntly.

Looks Far considered his reply for a long time. Then he shook his head. "I am not sure Man Above would agree with that."

"Would Looks Far Man desert me as well?" Medicine Wolf asked, his gaze hardening.

"I am not a deserter," Looks Far concluded. "I will stay, but I will not attack the stone lodge anymore, and there are many who will remain behind with me. You should consider that, my brother. It is something a leader should know."

"That those he leads will no longer follow?" Medicine Wolf asked bitterly. But Looks Far had already stood and was making his way back to the others.

Medicine Wolf let him go. The anger inside him blazed anew with the realization that the others would not follow him much longer. Not if he didn't bring them some sense of hope. A warrior was a man above all else, and he would not follow someone he didn't respect. Medicine Wolf knew that with each drop of Cheyenne blood spilled, with every hole each death gouged into the hearts of the living, their respect for him diminished.

He deliberately turned his back on the disgruntled warriors, knowing that as he did, he made himself as one alone.

"So be it," he whispered to Man Above.

CHAPTER 14

THE DAY BEGAN to wane. It grew warm inside the station, not unbearably so, but stuffy, and the waiting sawed at their nerves. Still, no one suggested opening the windows or venturing outside. Not after what had happened to Lester DeWeese.

Shortly after the midday meal, with no Cheyenne sighted for over an hour, Wilson sent DeWeese out with a pick and shovel to dig a grave for Abe Aaron. He wanted to get the gunfighter in the ground in case the siege worsened, or stretched into several days.

DeWeese, plodding with bowed head toward the slope behind the stable where they'd buried Shorty Phelps, never saw the arrow that took him high in the side, or the Indian who loosened it.

Clyde Cooper had been standing outside smoking a cigarette when DeWeese cried out in shock and pain, spinning under the arrow's impact. Clyde fast-drew an old Dance model revolver and peppered the trunk of the cottonwood tree where the Indian had lain in wait, but at seventy-five yards the distance was too great, even for a gunhand of Cooper's skills. The Indian fled, keeping in a low crouch and zigzagging among the trees until he was out of range. By the time Clint and Wilson showed up with their rifles, the Indian was out of sight.

They carried DeWeese inside and put him in bed with Wagner. Amos Booth had been stretched out on top of the blankets, dozing after the last Cheyenne attack. He scrambled out of bed when they brought DeWeese in, as if embarrassed to be caught napping.

Polly and Ruby looked after the young hostler while Booth dragged into the main room and slumped in the rocker. He looked tired, his face flushed and his eyes dull, but he refused to give in.

Ruby came out of the bedroom a half hour later with a wry smile on her lips. She paused in the doorway, her eyes searching out Clint. She said, "Well, we had a little better luck with this one."

"How is he?" Wilson asked with concern.

"He'll be fine," Ruby assured him. "The arrow missed everything that was vital and lodged between his ribs in back. We were able to cut it out with a lancet. He'll be on his feet again in no time."

Smiles flickered around the room. Even Cooper showed a degree of satisfaction in Ruby's announcement, as if saving the youth gave him some kind of stake in the boy's recovery. Ruby's gaze toured the room, then came back to Clint. He felt a warmth of unfamiliar emotions move through him as he returned her smile. The desire to be alone with her, to talk, to touch, had sharpened steadily with the hours.

Ruby went into the kitchen with a handful of bloody rags and the stained lancet. Leaving his rifle against the wall, Clint followed.

"You look tired," he offered, keeping his voice down for privacy's sake.

"We all are," Ruby replied. She looked into the main room. Booth's head was already tipped back against the rocker, and Grady was stretched out on a buffalo robe on the floor, his eyes closed. The others were scattered around the big room, mostly silent, lethargic in the sultry air.

"The waiting is worse than the attacks," she said softly.

"They'll give up after a while. It'll dawn on them sooner or later that they aren't going to tear these walls down, and that there are easier targets elsewhere."

"I would have thought they'd have figured that out yesterday," Ruby replied irritably. "Why do they keep hanging around? Is it personal?"

Something stirred. That was the only way Clint could describe it, the only way he'd ever been able to describe the physical sense of intuition—an awakening so deep inside himself that he seldom recognized what he felt clearly, not right off at least.

Ruby gave him a questioning look. "Clint, what is it?"

"Kane," Clint asked quietly. The old frontiersman was sitting cross-legged beside the front door, smoking his pipe. His eyes were narrowed lazily, but Clint had the uneasy feeling that he was far from sleep, that his gaze was on the two of them even now.

"What about him?" Ruby asked.

"What do you know about him?"

Ruby searched Clint's face, clearly puzzled. "Not much," she admitted. "We all boarded the stage at Leavenworth. There was another man then, a sallow-looking fellow in a dark suit, but he left us at Council Grove."

"Has Kane ever mentioned the Cheyenne, that he knew them, or that he was worried about them?"

Ruby was silent a minute, thinking back over the long hours they'd spent together inside the rocking coach. Finally she shook her head. "No, nothing, although it was obvious he became more nervous the farther west we traveled. After Pawnee Rock he was constantly looking out the windows, as if frightened of something. But we all were. With all the trouble that's been happening along the Smoky Hill Trail and on the Platte, we knew it was only a matter of time before it extended to other trails. I don't think anyone was surprised when the Cheyenne attacked, although we'd naturally hoped they wouldn't." She paused, giving him a moment, then said, "Tell me, Clint. What is it?"

Clint shook his head. "Maybe it's nothing. Just a feeling."

An uneasy, nagging feeling, but nothing he could put his finger on yet.

"You don't trust Kane." It was a statement that didn't require an answer.

"Do you? Or did you before yesterday?"

Again she was silent, trying to remember what she had felt toward Kane before her judgment of him had been colored by his actions of the day before. "No," she said at last. "I can remember thinking back at the Pawnee Rock Station, when it was dark, that I wouldn't want to be alone with him, that I feared him. Not what he might do to me personally, mind you. There were too many others around. But what he was capable of. That's what I feared, what he could do if he thought he was cornered, or trapped."

The way he is now, Clint thought.

Ruby was frowning. "You don't think Kane . . ."

"I don't know. He knows the Cheyenne. He's familiar with Indians. You can see it not only in his dress, but in the way he acts, the little mannerisms. Look at the way he's holding his pipe now, cradled on top of his arm. That's something he picked up from the plains tribes. You can see it in the way he walks too, soft and quietlike. I've been on the frontier all my life, trading with Indians since I was eighteen, but I still don't have those skills. You have to live with Indians a long time to pick up those habits."

"But he hates the Indians. He hates you because he thinks you're an—an Indian lover."

Clint smiled, catching the hitch in her voice. He turned away from Kane and looked at Ruby, sinking into the icy depth of her green eyes. "Do you think I'm an Indian lover?"

"I don't know. I only met you twenty-four hours ago, and we've hardly had a chance to get to know each other."

"Would it matter if I was?"

"No," she answered without hesitation.

Clint swallowed, wanting to take her into his arms, yet knowing it was impossible with so many others around.

"Clint . . . I . . ."

"Tonight maybe?"

She got a startled expression on her face, but then the surprise faded and she smiled. "Maybe. Where?"

"In the trees. Just a walk."

"Won't it be dangerous?"

"Probably. Will you come?"

"Yes," she answered.

A tangling web of emotions clutched at Clint—warmth and confusion, a hint of something new but powerful, a need he hadn't even realized existed until yesterday. Take it easy, he warned himself; take it slow and just see what happens.

Ruby looked at the bloody rags still in her hands, then dropped them into a pot of warm water. Watching the water spin and bubble while it slowly discolored, she said, "I'm not—"

"I know."

"Please, let me finish." She kept her eyes averted, her voice low. "The way I . . . dress, the way I act. Sometimes men think I'm . . . promiscuous. I was divorced when I was twenty. My husband left me for another woman, a girl actually, about Emma's age.

"My second husband was quite a bit older. I suppose I wanted the stability I'd envisioned a man like that could give. He was a businessman, and modestly wealthy. But I was only three years older than his oldest son."

She sighed, forcing herself to meet Clint's eyes. "When Edgar, my second husband, died . . . well, there was a lot of talk. Dirty talk. The children from his first wife contested the will in court and won, largely because I didn't mount much of a defense. I was allotted five hundred dollars and allowed to keep my personal belongings . . .

"I lived with my sister in Arrow Rock for about a year,

but as it turned out, that wasn't far enough away. I thought perhaps in Pueblo . . . I have an education, you see. I thought I could teach."

"That must've been a tough decision," Clint said gently.

"Yes. Now that I think about it, it was. But it was a good decision, the right decision." She shook her head then, smiling and changing the subject. "So, Mr. Clint Dawson, what's your story? A frontiersman all your life. An Indian trader. Tell me more."

He shrugged self-consciously, but felt an urge to talk, to share what seemed boring in retrospect. "There's not much to tell really. I left home when I was sixteen, looking for adventure. I've freighted and driven cattle. Worked for a trader for several years, dealing with the Pawnee and Osage. Once in a while we'd come out here to trade with the Cheyenne, Kiowa, and Wichita. Bill Hanks was the man's name. He was killed on the Cimarron, trying to trade with the Comanche, or so I was told. I was a partner in the firm by that time and had a separate outfit up on the Arkansas, looking for some Cheyenne.

"I was supposed to meet Bill at Bent's New Fort in eastern Colorado, but he never showed up. Some Comancheros who came wandering in had a few trade goods that looked familiar. They never denied the goods came from a white trader, but they said they got them from Comanche. No reason to doubt them, and they were free to trade with whoever they wanted. Lord knows that was what Bill was trying to do when he was killed. Those are the risks a man takes out here, but I guess it turned kind of sour for me after that. I packed up and went back to Leavenworth and sold out. When the railroad started west, I became a hunter, supplying the crews with meat, but that turned sour, too. I was on my way south looking for something new when I came on the stage yesterday."

"We're just a couple of pieces of driftwood, floating across the prairies."

He smiled, liking the sound of her words, the implications. "Something like that," he said. He started to lean toward her, then a sharp rap from the main room broke the moment.

Clint jerked his head around. Kane was leering at them from the far wall. The butt of his heavy butcher knife dropped between his fingers a second time to rap loudly on the wood floor.

Kane chuckled as the men around him snapped to attention. "Gotta keep awake, boys," he announced loudly. Looking at Clint, he added, "Ain't that right, sonny? Man's gotta keep his eyes peeled both front 'n back."

Clint nodded slowly. "That's right, old man. You've got to keep an eye peeled for backshooters all the time."

Kane's gaze hardened, the leer shifting into a mocking grin. "Smart boy, sonny. Mayhap you'll come through this with your hair on top of your head, after all, though I wouldn't take no wagers on it."

"That's enough, Kane," Booth growled. He heaved awkwardly to his feet, straightening his stiffened muscles with care. His face looked waxen in the fading light. Pulling a big, tin-plated pocket watch from his vest, he snapped the lid open and scowled at the face. "Six o'clock," he announced. "Time to change the guard."

It was getting dark. Time was running out.

Rusty felt Kane's gaze follow him into the kitchen. Polly and Ruby were in the bedroom, changing DeWeese's bandages. Clint, Wilson, Clyde, and Frank had gone out under arms to feed the stock. Emma sat alone at the kitchen table, kneading bread for the next day. Rusty knew Kane was impatient to make their move, but he didn't want to force Emma to come with him. It was a silly notion, but he wanted her to come of her own accord. Mostly, he thought, he wanted to see the look on John Wilson's face when his daughter rode out freely with a gunfighter and bank robber. And Wilson would know that before they left, Rusty vowed.

Emma looked up as Rusty rounded the long plank table, a half-hopeful, half-frightened expression giving her face a look of childlike innocence.

Rusty smiled. "I didn't think I was going to get a chance to talk to you again before I left."

"You're leaving!"

Rusty's confidence grew a fraction at the downfallen look on the girl's face. "After supper. Just me and Kane. And you too, if you want."

"Me? Oh, no, I—I couldn't."

"Are you going to tell me that you like it here?" Rusty countered.

Emma looked momentarily confused, then she shook her head. "No, but I can't just run off."

There was, Rusty reflected with a growing sense of triumph, a time in every game to bring out the hidden ace. "But that's what you were going to do," he said, catching her eye and holding it the way a snake held a mouse. Whispering, he said, "Shorty found your valise, hidden beside the stable."

She gave him a startled look, and Rusty's grin spread wide, like the wings of a bat in flight. "It had the letter you were going to leave behind for your folks. 'Dear Mama and Papa, I am going away for a while.' Sound familiar?"

"You had no right!" Emma gasped.

Rusty shrugged. "Didn't say I did, and I wouldn't have if I'd have known it was yours. But Shorty found it just after sunup this morning. It was him that brought me the letter. That's all I read, Emma. Just that first line. Then I realized it was yours and I put it back. That's part of the reason I shot Shorty this morning. To save your Papa and Dawson, sure, because Shorty was gonna kill them, but because he knew about your letter, too, and because he wanted to make fun of it with the boys. I wouldn't let him. I stopped him, Emma. Do you know why?"

Mutely, Emma shook her head.

"Because I love you. Does that sound silly?"

Emma looked as if she couldn't catch her breath. She glanced around wildly, reminding Rusty of a small animal cornered by something bigger and more dangerous. For a moment he was afraid she might panic and bolt, and that his chance to win her over without force might be lost. But then she took a deep breath, and although her lips trembled, she seemed calmer. "You don't know me, Mr. . . ."

Rusty played his hand smoothly, a game so old Emma must have thought she was inventing it herself. "Rusty," he said. "My real name is Richard, but I want you to call me Rusty."

His real name was Tom, but she didn't need to know that.

Emma swallowed. "Okay, Richard . . . Rusty. But I don't know you. I couldn't just run off. It ain't proper."

"Listen to me, Emma. I love you. I fell in love with you last night and I love you so much, it's near paining me to death right now. But I can't stay. I've got business out West, in the goldfields." Rusty shifted gears. "My brother's struck it rich in Idaho, and I'm going up to help him sell the mine. He's giving me half, Emma. We could go anywhere with that kind of money. Anywhere. St. Louis, New York, London, Paris. You'll have pretty clothes, fancy carriages."

She lifted her hands, covered in dough but reddened beneath, and Rusty sensed her dissatisfaction, the hopelessness of her existence here. He took her hands, rubbing his thumbs through the dough. "You won't ever have to wash another dish as long as you live. You can have maids and cooks, and we could go to parties at night and eat in fancy restaurants where waiters in ties and jackets will serve you."

"I . . . I can't. I just couldn't."

"Listen to me," Rusty said earnestly. "Listen, Emma. You ain't gonna escape this place by slipping away on the next stage. It just ain't gonna happen. Your pa's gonna saddle a mule and catch up before you reach the next station. He'll bring you back here like you were some little know-nothing girl, some kid that ain't growed up yet. And he'll keep you that way until you get so sick of it you'll marry some hayseed like DeWeese or Shaw just to get away. But you won't be getting away, because whoever you marry will be some bumpkin your old man picked out for you, someone he can keep on his leash. That way he can keep you on his leash, too, until he dies and you're an old woman with a dozen kids and withered dreams.

"Don't let those dreams die, Emma. You're a woman, a beautiful woman. Don't wither up like some pumpkin blossom wilting in the sun. Take a chance, girl. Listen to your heart singing. Hear it? Listen to it."

Emma looked as if she might faint. She squeezed her eyes shut and held onto Rusty's hands.

Rusty's grip tightened. "Right after supper, Emma. Be ready."

"I don't know if I can," she whispered.

"You can. Because you know that if you don't, you'll die just like a blossom on a vine."

"Like a blossom on a vine," she echoed.

CHAPTER 15

THERE WAS NO plan, no signal to begin.

When supper was finished, Rusty pushed back from the table and looked across the room to where Kane stood with his plate in one hand, his spoon in the other, the Henry rifle caught in the crook of his arm. Catching the old man's eye, Rusty winked and stood, sliding his Colts smoothly from their well-oiled holsters.

"Yeehaw, boys!" Rusty hollered, snapping a shot at the kettle of stew sitting in the middle of the table. The kettle jumped and spun, spraying a thick, rich broth over the time-scarred planks. Kicking his chair away, he backpedaled across the kitchen, keeping one revolver on Clint and the other on Wilson.

Kane choked on a piece of buffalo meat and dropped his plate with a clatter, splashing his half-finished stew over the beaded toes of his moccasins. Jacking a round into the Henry's chamber, he swung the muzzle toward the group gathered in the kitchen. Glaring at Rusty, his dark eyes blazing, Kane spat, "God almighty, boy, are you crazy?"

"Crazy is the best way to live, you old fool," Rusty shouted happily. He cocked his right-hand revolver, the one trained on Clint. "Go get the others," he told Kane. "I can handle this bunch."

"What the hell is this, Cantrell?" Booth demanded, struggling to his feet. Rusty debated killing the man just to avoid argument, then decided against it; the arrowhead still embedded in Booth's shoulder seemed to be doing that just fine.

Kane pushed away from the wall and hurried into the main bedroom after DeWeese and Wagner. Clyde stood uncertainly at the door to the storage room, his sawed-off shotgun cocked and leveled, although he didn't look like he was sure which way to point it.

"Go tell Frank to keep his eye peeled," Rusty told Clyde. "Tell him we're leaving, but to just stay where he is until someone comes to get him."

"Where the hell we goin'?" Clyde blurted.

"Just tell Frank to keep his post, then go fetch the kid," Rusty said. Frank was manning the southeast bastion, while young Jack Wilson kept watch in the northwest bastion. Wagner and DeWeese had been awakened by Rusty's shot, and Kane was herding them into the main room before Clyde could duck through the storage room door.

"By God, I asked a question," Booth sputtered.

"Me'n the boys have decided it's time to leave you kind folks," Rusty replied sardonically. "We do want you to know your hospitality was appreciated though, and that we don't intend to steal any more than we can carry."

Wilson, his face burning with rage, started to rise. Rusty plowed a slug into the table just in front of him. "Sit down, Papa," he said in a razor-edged voice.

Clyde delivered Rusty's message to Cassidy in the storage room and hurried across the main room to the northwest bastion just in time to catch Jack Wilson coming through the door. Clyde knocked the Springfield from the kid's hands, then cuffed him up side his head for good measure. "Git into the kitchen," he commanded gruffly.

Looking more stunned from the unexpectedness of Cooper's violence than the actual blow, young Wilson stumbled into the kitchen. Motioning with the muzzle of his shotgun, Clyde snarled to Shaw and DeWeese. "You, too. Move it."

When everyone was gathered in the kitchen, Rusty said,

"Okay, Kane, go get their weapons and pile 'em in the storage room."

The old frontiersman moved quickly through the group, lifting revolvers and knives from the men. He made a second trip for the rifles, muskets, and carbines they had kept close to their sides through the meal, then paused beside Ruby, leaning close to snicker in her face. "How 'bout you, honey? You got anything hid out that ol' Kane oughta know about?"

"Leave her alone," Clint snapped with such fury Kane actually stepped back.

Rusty laughed. "Goddamn, old man, you've already taken his rifle and pistol away. You still afraid of him?"

Kane's face filled with an anger that had been building for two days. Stepping swiftly forward, he drove the Henry's brass butt into Clint's stomach. Shock and pain exploded across Clint's face, and the air burst from his lungs. He grunted in a strangled voice and staggered back against the wall, sliding slowly to the floor. Both Wilson and Booth jerked as if they wanted to go to Clint's aid, but Rusty merely lifted the twin muzzles of his revolvers and they stopped.

"Just settle down, boys," Rusty warned. "No sense in anyone getting hurt."

"We ought to kill a couple of 'em anyway," Clyde growled. "For Shorty and Abe's sake."

Rusty chuckled. "Well, that may be true, ol' buddy, but I'm the one who killed Shorty, and it was Indians who killed Abe. It don't hardly seem fair to make these kind folks pay for that. Especially after feeding us as well as they have. As I recollect, you were getting mighty hungry before we rode in."

"I reckon we paid for our keep," Clyde grumbled.

"Well, that is a good point, but I still ain't hankering to kill anyone if we don't have to."

"I ain't said *I* wouldn't," Kane snapped, pushing free of

the prisoners to stand beside Rusty. "I'd like a piece of that bastard right there," he said, pointing to Clint, who was on his knees, leaning against the wall and gasping hoarsely for breath.

Rusty laughed. "Hang onto that stew, Dawson," he called. "You wouldn't want to insult these fine ladies here." He looked at Emma and smiled.

"Watch yourself, Cantrell," Wilson warned.

"Oh, I always watch myself," Rusty replied, grinning. "That's why I'm standing here with the guns, and you're standing there looking like a goddamn fool.

"Clyde, go saddle the horses. All of 'em. Kane's coming with us."

"Right." Keeping the shotgun with him, Clyde went to the front door, peered cautiously outside, then ducked into the darkness.

"What do you think, Kane? Any Cheyenne out there?"

"I guess we'll know soon enough," Kane replied.

Rusty smiled but didn't reply. He figured an Indian wouldn't want to fight at night any more than a white man, although it never hurt to send someone else out first.

"I thought it was just you and me?" Kane said, watching him closely.

"Don't worry about it. We'll be fine."

"I ain't aimin' to become no outlaw," Kane argued. "I ain't joinin' your gang."

"What?" Emma appeared shaken by the words *outlaw* and *gang*.

"I don't have a gang anymore," Rusty answered flatly. Looking at Emma, he said, "Time to change into some riding clothes, girl."

Fear crossed her face. Wilson stood, jerking up from the table as if spring-loaded. "I'll kill you, Cantrell, before I let you take my little girl."

"She ain't your little girl anymore, Wilson. She's my woman."

Polly Wilson blanched, and Ruby gasped. "My God, Cantrell, don't you have any decency?" Ruby asked.

Rusty grinned wickedly. "Why sure, I got buckets of decency. That's why Emma and I are gonna get married . . . later on."

"You're an animal, Cantrell!" Ruby cried.

The humor left Rusty's face. His finger tightening ever so slightly on the revolver's trigger, he said, "Don't push it, Ruby. I could get mad."

"You are mad. Can't you see that? Can't you see this is crazy?"

Rusty's vision hazed, and the walls seemed to close in. The voices of the others—John and Polly Wilson, Jack, Grady Shaw—blurred into a solid roaring that filled his head. He choked out a curse and lifted his revolver, firing into the ceiling.

The blast of the Colt silenced them. Bark and dirt showered the tabletop, then dribbled to a halt. Slowly, the roaring in Rusty's ears faded. He blinked and swallowed, and his gaze settled on Emma. "Get changed into your riding clothes," he said tautly. "Do it now, girl, or I'm gonna kill your sweet papa here."

"Please, Mr. Cantrell. I . . . I've changed my mind. I don't want to go—"

"I said git!" Rusty shrieked. He lifted his left-hand Colt. The narrow blade of the front sight settled on John Wilson's chest, the third button down from the neck. "I said, git," he repeated softly.

Sobbing, Emma moved to comply.

Clint was trying to stand, his eyes narrowed in grim determination, but before he could gain his feet Kane hurried in, bringing his rifle down in a sweeping blow. The solid crack of the Henry's wooden stock on Clint's skull filled the kitchen with a terrifying crunch. Clint grunted and flopped limply to the floor.

"Clint!" Ruby screamed. *"Clint!"* She started toward him,

but Kane grabbed her arm and jerked her back. "Not so fast, missy. You're comin' with us." He chuckled crudely, giving her a shake. "You kin be the little girl's chaperone."

Ruby struggled desperately, crying, "Let me go, Kane! Let me go!"

Kane slapped her face, hard. Ruby cried out and her knees buckled. She might have fallen if not for Kane's grip on her arm. He jerked her roughly to her feet, snarling, "Git in there with the young'un and change into somethin' that'll hold up on the trail." He let her go, and she stepped back, staring at him in horror.

"Unnerstand me, missy," Kane continued. "I don't much give a goddamn if I gotta drag you along buck naked. It's your choice."

Numbly, on leaden feet, Ruby stepped past him and followed Emma into the smaller bedroom.

"Cantrell, if you do this I swear I'll hound you to hell," Wilson grated. "I'll kill you in ways that'll make you beg for a bullet. I swear to that, no matter what it takes."

"Those are bold words for an unarmed man."

"Please, mister," Polly choked, her stern countenance breaking at last. "Please don't take my little girl. She's—she's just a child."

Rusty grinned. "Well, ma'am, don't you worry about that. She'll grow up real fast."

"You sonofabitch," Wilson breathed hoarsely. "You sonofabitch. If you harm—"

Rusty waved the muzzle of his Colt. "Uh-uh. Just save it, Wilson. Get shot now, and who's gonna come after your little girl?"

"That's the only reason, the only reason, you damn bastard."

Laughing, Rusty said, "You do beat all. Maybe I ought to just plug you here and not have to worry about you."

"You can't kill us all."

"Do you know how many men I've killed, Wilson? Do you think a few more's gonna make any difference?"

"No. I have no doubt that you're a killer, Cantrell. I knew that when I saw you ride in, hiding behind the others. You are a coward to the core. You kill because you don't have the courage to face a man any other way. Inside, your guts are—"

Rusty's Colt roared, the slug tearing into the meat of Wilson's thigh and spinning him to the side. He grabbed for the edge of the table and fell over it, sucking his breath in, his face paling.

"You couldn't let it rest, could you?" Rusty shouted. "You couldn't just bide your time. You *dumb* sonofabitch. You stupid dumb goddamn . . ."

The words trailed off abruptly, and Rusty whipped his Colt up, snapping a shot at Jack Wilson's head. The bullet slammed into the stone wall behind the boy, splintering lead that ricocheted wildly. The younger Wilson cried out and grabbed his neck, jumping as pieces of lead stung his thin flesh. Rusty laughed harshly. "You wouldn't be the first kid, either," he told the boy. "Women, kids. It don't matter to me. Never did."

"Please," Wagner gasped in his reedy, consumptive voice. "I beg of you, show them some mercy."

"Shut up, you English bastard," Rusty said shakily. He leaned against the counter, the Colts suddenly heavy in his hands. "From now on, no one talks. Understand?" He looked at Kane and was gratified to see fear on the old frontiersman's face as well. "That goes for you too, *partner*. Just let it drop until Clyde gets back with the horses."

An uneasy silence settled over the station. Rusty's anger began to fade, but erratically, the way a blaze dies slowly. His outburst shamed him, the shame bringing a renewed anger.

The front door creaked open and Clyde came in with several sets of saddlebags draped over his free arm. His gaze swept the room, took in Clint lying unconscious on the floor and Wilson slumped over the table with his hand clamped to his thigh, his fingers bloody and his face smeared with broth. Clyde glanced questioningly at Rusty, but held his tongue.

"You get 'em?" Rusty asked in a strangled tone.

"Tied up at the rail out front," Clyde replied.

"Put some grub together. Get that broad-assed bitch to help." Rusty pointed to Polly with his Colt.

Sobbing quietly, Polly allowed Clyde to lead her into the storage room. Edging closer, Kane said, "What's going on, Cantrell? You didn't say—"

"Shut up, Kane. Just shut up. I have to think."

The prisoners were silent, watching Rusty cautiously. Wilson had sagged into a chair, but Booth and Wagner still stood, Wagner's legs trembling with weakness.

"You all are a pretty sight," Rusty said. He forced a smile, and added, "Why don't you sit down before you fall down? Amos, have a seat."

"I'm fine right here," the driver said quietly.

Rusty's gaze hardened. "I said sit down!"

Grudgingly, Booth pulled out a chair and sat. Wagner sank onto a bench, propping his elbow on the table and holding his forehead.

Rusty motioned to DeWeese. "You too, plowboy. Plunk it right there at the table. I don't want you passing out on me."

DeWeese sat without argument. Grady Shaw and young Jack Wilson remained standing, their backs to the kitchen wall. Rusty grinned, taking in the group's weakened condition, their wounds and illnesses. He told himself that he had done right in shooting Wilson and allowing Kane to club Clint. Even his symbolic wounding of the boy drove his message across. They were weak, all of them, and he was strong. He wanted them to remember that and to appreciate the gift of life that he would grant them if they behaved.

Clyde and Polly came out of the storeroom, and Clyde took the bulging saddlebags outside to strap them in place while Polly joined her husband at the table. It was another five minutes before Ruby and Emma reappeared. Both had changed into riding skirts and high-necked blouses. Ruby's skirt was obviously borrowed. It was a little tight, a little short, but better than riding in a dress, Rusty figured. Emma wore a narrow-brimmed felt hat with a drawstring pulled tight under her chin. Ruby wore a plain, sun-faded pioneer bonnet, pushed off the back of her head.

Rusty nodded approvingly as they entered the room. "You're showing more sense than your papa, Emma," he said, pleased. "You'll need that hat tomorrow." He looked at Ruby and winked. "You don't look like the bonnet-wearing type, but maybe I'm wrong."

"Have your fun, Cantrell. The law will catch up with you soon enough."

"Darlin', the law's been trying to catch up with me for a good many years. It ain't done it yet."

Clyde came back, frowning when he spotted the two women. "They going? I didn't saddle enough horses for everyone."

Rusty held a finger to his lips. "Shhh. I decided we ain't taking Frank. He'd just be deadweight where we're going."

"Huh?" Clyde looked confused, his tiny eyes narrowing suspiciously. Rusty couldn't help a flitting glance to the shotgun held in Clyde's right hand, its barrel slanted toward the floor. He knew he would have to tread lightly now. Clyde was a man slow to arouse, but stubborn once he got an idea lodged in his mind, and he was wary now, sensing betrayal.

Rusty glanced at the old frontiersman. "What about it, Kane? Is it safe to ride yet?"

"I reckon now's about the best time," Kane replied.

"Sun's down and the moon ain't up yet. There'll be Injuns about, don't you doubt that for a cat's second. But if'n we slip out quietlike, keep t' the shadows as much as possible, we oughta be able t' slip over the ridge 'fore they know we're gone. I wouldn't try it, I didn't think we stood a chance."

"Damnit, man," Wilson said with anguish. "It's bad enough that you'd risk your own necks on such a desperate plan, but don't risk a woman and child."

Kane snorted derisively. "That redheaded heifer there could be our ticket outta here, it comes t' it. Injuns set a heap of store in forkin' a white woman. Could be they'd trade us passage outta here for one of these girlies."

Emma gasped, and Polly moaned and seemed to sink into the table. Amos Booth growled, "You'd trade a white woman to a Cheyenne—"

"Shut up," Rusty ordered. He glanced at the frontiersman. "Time to go. Kane, keep an eye on these folks. Clyde and I will get the women mounted." He winked lewdly. "On their horses, I mean."

"Mr. Cantrell," Emma wailed. "Please! Please! I don't want to go."

"Get your valise, girl, and quit your whining. You're going, so you might as well stop fighting it."

"Why don't you leave her, Cantrell?" Ruby said abruptly, stepping forward and throwing her shoulders back to pull the fabric of her blouse tight across her breasts. "A little girl bawling for her ma all the way is just going to get on your nerves." She stopped, swallowed, and went on. "Besides, I'm enough . . . woman . . . for all of you."

Rusty laughed in wonder. "Why Ruby, you're blushing. Maybe I misjudged you. Maybe you ain't as experienced as I figured you were. But that was a noble effort, and I do admire you for it. Let's go."

"Bastard," Ruby murmured.

"Uh-huh."

Clyde led them to the door. Rusty herded the women before him. Emma was whimpering softly, and for a moment Rusty considered Ruby's suggestion to leave her behind. Then stubbornness killed the thought, and he thumped the back of her head with his fingers. "Shut up now."

They slipped outside, pulling the door closed behind them, and paused in a group on the stoop. A dusting of stars sprinkled the ink-shaded canopy of the sky, a frosted backdrop to the silhouette of Rocky Top to the north. But the moon hadn't yet come up and Rusty knew they were well shielded among the trees, invisible to even the most prying eyes of the Cheyenne. Still, a chill ran down his spine like cold, tickling fingers. *A man just never knows*, he told himself.

"Which ones you want 'em mounted on?" Clyde asked in a hushed voice.

"Put Ruby on Abe's horse. I'll put Emma on Shorty's."

He took the girl's arm and led her to the gelding Shorty had chosen for his long-distance runner. It was a tall, well-muscled sorrel with a deep chest and a broad head. Rusty checked the cinch with his free hand. Emma was trembling, her teeth chattering. Rusty pulled her roughly against him. Leaning close, he hissed, "Listen up. If you're scared, that's fine. I was scared the day I left home, too. But I didn't scream about it, and you ain't going to either. There're Cheyenne out there just waiting for us to make a wrong move, and if you think you've got it bad now, you ain't thinking what it'll be like if them Indians catch you."

"Please, Rusty. Please."

Rusty shook her impatiently. "You don't listen worth a damn, do you?" he said in a wondering tone. "Well, you'll learn."

"Please."

Rusty laughed, mimicking her. "Please!" he squeaked. "Like a little mouse. Please!"

"My God, Cantrell, are you going to torture her now?" Ruby asked from her mount.

"Get on the horse," Rusty ordered the girl. He had to help her mount, and once she was in the saddle he thought she would tumble off the other side. Her limbs were weak as rags, and he swore and pulled Shorty's picket rope off the saddle. He quickly tied Emma's ankles to the stirrups, running the rope under the horse's belly. Clyde did the same with Ruby. They left the bridles on both mounts, but knotted the reins to the headstall. "We'll lead 'em until they decide they won't try to run off," Rusty told Clyde.

When they finished they stood back to admire their handiwork. "That ought to hold 'em," Clyde said with satisfaction. While Clyde studied the women, Rusty slipped his Colt free.

"You were a tolerable friend, all things considered," Rusty said gently.

"Huh?" Clyde started to turn toward him. Rusty brought the butt of his Colt down hard against his partner's head. Clyde grunted and fell with a dull plop, the shotgun bouncing from his fingers. Emma began to cry softly, but Ruby merely snorted.

"Don't do this, Cantrell. Don't—"

Rusty slammed his Colt against Ruby's knee, and she cried out, jackknifing forward over the saddle horn. "I want you to shut up now," Rusty said patiently. "From here on, you'll do what I say."

He went back inside. The prisoners hadn't moved, but Kane had edged closer to the front door. Rusty smiled tiredly. "What's the matter, Kane. Don't trust me?"

"S—sure," Kane stammered. "Sure, I trust you. Jus' wanted t' be ready, is all."

Rusty shook his head, glancing at the prisoners. "The first person—man, woman, or boy—to poke his head out the door gets it blown off. Remember that."

He turned and went out the front door, Kane almost tripping on his heels.

CHAPTER 16

HE SWAM SLOWLY upward, struggling weakly toward the circle of light that shone like a distant lantern. Voices guided him, kept him on course. Muted and rumbling, like the vibration of distant hooves pounding the hard sod of the prairie. A buffalo herd on the move. He could see them now, smell them. The pungent odor of shaggy hides tingeing the wind.

But there was no wind, no running buffalo. Clint's eyes fluttered open. He lay on his back on a buffalo robe, the glow of firelight dancing along dark rafters. The mumble of voices came from his right. He tried to move his head in that direction, but the pain was too sharp, too swift; it clubbed his eyes shut again.

Footsteps rapped a dull cadence on the wood floor, pounding even louder in Clint's skull. He forced his eyes open again, careful not to move him head. John Wilson hove into his field of vision, his unshaven face drawn and haggard in the harsh light, his eyes filled with pain. Squatting awkwardly, he said, "How're you doing, Clint?"

"What . . . happened?" He had to try twice to get the words out.

"How much do you remember?"

Clint tried to think back, but his thoughts were hazy, as tangled as old harness dumped in a heap on a stable floor. Only slowly did the memories emerge, separating themselves from the throbbing knot of pain that fogged his mind—the kettle of stew spinning wildly atop the table; Rusty Cantrell's cackling, high-pitched laughter; Ruby's scream as if from a long way away. Somewhere in the deeper recesses, a gunshot seemed to echo. "Not much, I guess," he managed.

Wilson sighed, rubbing his chin. "Cantrell turned on us," he said flatly. "He and Kane took Emma and Ruby."

Clint blinked, struggling to comprehend Wilson's words. Panic welled up in him. He took a deep, shaky breath, and said, "Where? Where'd he . . . take them?"

"South. My boy followed them as far as the edge of the trees. They turned into a gulch that'll take them over the ridge and out of sight. As far as we know, the Cheyenne haven't spotted them yet, but it's only a matter of time, once the sun comes up."

"When?" It was getting easier, this process of questioning, of bringing himself back from the snarled web of unconsciousness.

"Early last night, right after supper. It's almost dawn now."

"We'll have to . . . have to . . ."

"Go after them?" Wilson said, patting Clint's shoulder. "We will. Don't worry about that. But I was shot in the leg. Booth is racked with fever; he wouldn't last two miles on the back of a horse. Both Wagner and DeWeese are too weak, and Jack is too young. That leaves me, maybe Grady . . . and you, if you're up to it."

Clint nodded and licked his lips. "I'm up to it."

"One thing. We're short on horses. They left Clyde Cooper's roan and your two, but everything else is mules. Mules'll last longer, but they wouldn't be able to keep up with horses. Not these mules, anyway. They're too big and brawny."

"What about the rest of Cantrell's men?"

"Rusty clubbed Cooper in the yard and left Cassidy behind in the bastion keeping watch. We tied up both of them and put them in the storage room."

Clint tried to rise, but Wilson pushed him back. "Take it

easy, Dawson. It's too late to slip out of here undetected. We're going to have to come up with some kind of plan."

"We can't wait long. They've already got a night's lead on us."

"I know, but if we're going to follow them we'll have to do it around the Cheyenne."

"Damnit, man, they've got—" Clint shut up abruptly. They had Ruby, all right. But they also had Emma. He'd forgotten that for a moment. "John, I'm—I'm sorry about your little girl. I—"

"Drop it," Wilson interrupted, his voice torn with pain. "We'll get her back." He patted Clint's shoulder clumsily. "We'll get both of them back. I'll swear to God on that."

Medicine Wolf stared at the slow curl of smoke drifting upward from the cooling ashes of his fire. Sun still lingered in the land of the Osages, but soon He would begin His journey across the rippled plains. Soon He would see the shame that engulfed Medicine Wolf.

The Appaloosa stamped its hoof impatiently, breaking Medicine Wolf's meditation. He lifted his gaze lovingly to the short-coupled war pony he'd stolen from the Nez Perce three winters before. The Appaloosa whickered questioningly, its big doe eyes liquid, intelligent, its nostrils flaring. A smile like a crooked fissure in a copper cliff broke the somber countenance of Medicine Wolf's face, pushing down the sense of betrayal he felt toward the others.

Only Looks Far Man, Lost His Horse, Running Elk, Cuts His Hair, and a handful of others remained. Fewer than the fingers that a man carried on two hands. The rest had ridden off in search of easier prey, giving up their resolve to capture the traitor White Hawk.

Medicine Wolf's smile turned suddenly bitter. "Are they not as White Hawk himself?" he asked aloud, speaking to the Appaloosa.

The spotted pony lifted its head and snorted, but it was

Looks Far who answered. "They grew weary of seeing their brothers die, my friend. It was not you they deserted, but the battle against the stone walls where White Hawk burrows."

Medicine Wolf's features twisted. Lifting his voice, he shouted, "I am Medicine Wolf. I am a warrior. I will not tuck my tail between my legs like a cur and slink away from the difficult path."

"Perhaps they didn't believe in your medicine, Medicine Wolf," a new voice suggested.

Medicine Wolf jumped to his feet, facing the man who had spoken. His name was Lucky In Love, and he was a tall, burly warrior with curly dark hair. His mother had been a black woman, traded from the Kiowas many seasons before, after being captured from a plantation in the land of the Comanches that the white-eyes called Texas.

Lucky In Love strode forward, his narrowed eyes haughty, mocking. "Maybe they asked themselves, 'Where is the white wolf that guides our war chief? Where is his medicine?'" The others had been sitting around a separate fire, waiting in silence. They looked up now, curious but still neutral.

"Why have you stayed, if you do not trust my leadership?" Medicine Wolf asked bluntly.

"To seek a scalp that glows in the light of Sun like fresh snow."

"Then we are of one thought."

"No, I would never allow so many to die for my own vanity."

"It is easy to lead from the back of the lodge," Looks Far murmured just loud enough for the others to hear.

"You are of the People," Medicine Wolf said to Lucky In Love. "A warrior leads or follows of his own will."

Lucky In Love seemed startled by Medicine Wolf's words; his eyes narrowed. "It was you, Medicine Wolf, who

Blue Man Limping and the others appointed leader. I will not turn deaf to their wishes."

Looks Far sniffed and looked away, a slightly contemptuous smile turning up the corners of his lips. Medicine Wolf fought his own smile. Lucky In Love coveted the rank of war chief, but was reluctant to defy the decision of the elders who had spoken in favor of Medicine Wolf. But in hesitating, he had revealed his own doubts, losing any chance to snatch the reins of leadership from Medicine Wolf's grasp.

A surge of relief moved through Medicine Wolf. Lucky In Love, sensing the opportunity he'd lost, seemed on the verge of taking another tack when the drumming of hooves from upstream broke his concentration. Glancing over his shoulder, Medicine Wolf saw Lost His Horse racing across the dusty flat to avoid the shallow curve of an oxbow. His arm flashed as he quirted his pony, and Medicine Wolf turned his back on Lucky In Love.

Lost His Horse rode into the trees without slowing, pulling his lathered mount to a dirt-showering stop at the last instant.

"White Hawk has left," Lost His Horse blurted, throwing himself from the pad saddle.

Medicine Wolf's eyes narrowed. He stepped forward and closed his hand over the peak of Lost His Horse's shoulder, digging his fingers into the flesh. "My brother is sure of this?"

Lost His Horse's head bobbed excitedly. "The tracks were found this morning, in the big coulee that runs toward the land of the Comanche. Four riders. One of them was White Hawk. Two others were women."

Medicine Wolf smiled wryly. "Then it was Wet Otter who found their trail."

Lost His Horse looked embarrassed. "Yes. Only Wet Otter can read sign as well as the elders or tell who rides a horse by the trail that horse leaves."

"Wet Otter waits?" Medicine Wolf asked.

"Yes, at the head of the coulee, where it enters the trees."

Medicine Wolf examined the lay of the land in his mind, then nodded. He knew the place. He turned to Looks Far and smiled. "My brother's words are good. The badger has fled his burrow."

Looks Far said, "I will get my pony."

They were a motley-looking bunch. Wilson gimped into the main room with his bedroll slung over his shoulder, DeWeese's stubby .56 Spencer tucked under his arm. He'd changed into clean overalls that were baggy enough not to irritate his bandaged thigh, but hadn't taken time to wash or shave. The gray stubble on his chin, coupled with the weariness of the past couple of days and the worry of the past night, had added twenty years to the station manager's appearance.

Grady Shaw stood uncertainly beside the front door, silent and maybe a little frightened, but too stubborn to acknowledge it. He'd taken the bandage off his head, but the torn, barely-scabbed flesh was still too tender to take the constriction of a hat. His cornshuck yellow hair was cropped close, but ruffled. He held onto the barrel of Emma's Springfield with his right hand, its butt resting on the floor beside his boots.

Clint leaned against the table in the kitchen, drinking a cup of coffee. His head still throbbed and there was a lump the size of a walnut above his right ear, but except for a lingering queasiness he felt all right.

Conversation had flowed erratically around the cavernous room while Wilson and his wife retired to Emma's bedroom for a few last words in private. It ground to an uncomfortable halt when he returned. Amos Booth, sitting in the rocker by the fireplace, struggled to his feet.

He turned to Wagner, but was unable to meet the Englishman's unblinking gaze.

"Cheer up, old chap," Wagner said gently. "It was a fair decision. Besides, this could be a grand adventure yet, something to reminisce over in a pub somewhere down the line, eh?"

"Sure," Booth said gruffly, thrusting a calloused hand forward. "Sure." He looked like he wanted to say more, but couldn't. Turning away, he walked across the room like a man defeated.

"I would have insisted anyway," Wagner told the room in general. "It's only logical, you see. We couldn't very well have had young Jack here going, now could we?"

Something inside Clint knotted suddenly, and he swallowed back the protest that formed in his throat. They were trapped inside the station while the Cheyenne flitted back and forth among the trees at the upper end of the grove. It was only a matter of time before they discovered the story of Cantrell's escape written plainly in the grass, assuming they hadn't already. Somehow they had to lure them away from the trees long enough for Wilson, Clint, and Grady Shaw to slip out. It was Wagner who had suggested drawing straws.

"Short man creates a diversion, eh?"

Only it had been a setup from the beginning, Clint knew. While the others continued to argue in the main room, Wagner went into the storage room to find a broom, peeling three straws from the bundle. Coming back with the straws clutched in his hand, Wagner had announced the rules himself. "Clint, John, Grady, and young Jack are exempt. Jack is still a boy, and the others are the best men to follow Kane and Cantrell, and therefore have the best chance of rescuing the women. We shall, of course, exclude Mrs. Wilson." He'd smiled graciously to Polly Wilson, sitting like a stone in the kitchen, then turned back to the others. "Shall we?" he'd asked, extending his deadly bouquet toward Booth.

Booth angrily snatched one of the straws from Wagner's hand, then refused to look at it. Wagner pivoted and Lester DeWeese edged reluctantly forward, licking at his lips. Using a thumb and forefinger, his hands hovered briefly over the two remaining straws, then chose the one farthest from Wagner.

Only Clint saw Wagner's quick sleight of hand, the forward snap of his pinky finger that slid the remaining straw from sight and pushed the second straw into its place.

"Well," Wagner sighed, pulling the eyes of the others away from the trembling straw in DeWeese's hand. "It would appear I have drawn the winning hand."

"Damnit," Booth exploded. "You're not going, Wagner. Not while you're the responsibility of the L&P."

"Its responsibility, old chap, but hardly its property. I hereby absolve your honorable Leavenworth and Pueblo Line of all liability, with everyone here as my witness."

"It won't wash," Booth fumed. "By God, I won't stand for it. It would be like murder!" He glared at Wagner, but the Englishman merely shrugged tacitly. Clint sympathized with Booth's frustration, but he knew they had to think of the women first. Not just of what was happening to them now, with Kane and Cantrell, but what might happen if they fell into the hands of the Cheyenne. In the end, they didn't have any choice. Even Booth knew that.

Clint remained in the kitchen, the cup of coffee starting to cool. Wagner made his rounds with a quiet dignity, his smile small but genuine. When he finally worked his way into the kitchen to wish Clint luck and speed, Clint could barely speak. "You're all right, Jerome," he managed after a false start. "Amos was right, you've got grit enough for ten men."

"I shall cherish that compliment," Wagner said gently.

He turned away, and Clint set his coffee aside. The Whitworth was leaning against the table beside him. He picked it up and followed Wagner toward the front door.

They exited cautiously and made their way around the station until the upper end of the grove was in full view. Less than half a dozen Cheyenne were still milling within easy range of the Whitworth's heavy slug, but they seemed unconcerned, their attention focused elsewhere.

"They've found Cantrell's trail," Wilson predicted grimly. Only he, Clint, and Wagner had left the building. The rest remained inside, not wanting to draw the attention of the Cheyenne just yet. Clint doubted if they would have noticed anyway. They were working themselves into a frenzy, whipping their ponies back and forth, chattering angrily.

"They appear to be waiting for someone," Wagner observed.

"They won't wait forever," Wilson replied. Then the implication of his words struck him and he glanced guiltily at Wagner.

"Perfectly all right," Wagner said kindly. "We mustn't dally." He led the way to the corral, but remained to one side while Clint and Wilson saddled and bridled the horses, conserving his waning strength. He carried only his revolver and Grady's shotgun. Amos had wanted him to take several revolvers, and try to make a wide circle and fight his way back to the station. But Wagner refused to even consider it.

"My goal is to lure the Cheyenne away from the station. I shall do my utmost. As *far* away as your fastest mule will carry me."

When the horses were readied, Wilson led a big gray jack into the stable. "Think you can handle this one, Jerome?" he asked.

Wagner studied the animal with a humorous expression. "A bit of white around the eye, eh?"

"He'll take the bit in his teeth and go," Wilson told him. "So just let him. Going east, the next station is forty miles, more or less. You can make that by noon if you keep ahead of the Indians."

"I dare say this brute appears to have the capability. But does he have the speed?"

"I don't know," Wilson admitted glumly. "But he's the fastest animal on the place, after Clint's dun and Clyde Cooper's roan."

"Then we shall see, eh?"

"Hell, you don't have to look so all-fired cheerful about it," Clint said.

"Ah, but why shouldn't I feel cheerful? My lungs are rested and my body has recovered from its ordeal of the past several days. I am a dying man, offered a last chance at glory. I relish the opportunity, believe me." His eyes misted suddenly, and he smiled. "I am going to die a hero, Clint, on the wild American frontier. I have left instructions for Amos to return my diary to my people in Bristol, filling in the final page as he sees fit. I will be a legend there, don't you see?"

Clint nodded. "You'll be a legend here too," he said thickly.

Smiling, Wagner said, "All the better, then. But please, help me mount. This is such a tall animal, and I've never been much of a horseman."

"You won't have to be on ol' Rufus here," Wilson said, patting the big gray's neck. "Just put him on the road heading east and hang on."

"Splendid, then." He stepped up to the gray, his face inches from the jack's whiskered muzzle, seeming to communicate without words. Then he moved around to the side. Clint gave him a boost into the saddle, surprised by Wagner's frailness, the slight trembling of his muscles. He wondered briefly if Wagner could hang on for forty miles, even assuming the mule could stay ahead of the Indians' ponies for that long, then pushed the thought from his mind. He didn't suppose it would matter. Wagner would do what he could, and when he fell no man there would wonder if he could have done more.

They shook hands a final time, then Wilson opened the gate and Wagner trotted the mule into the clear.

The Cheyenne spotted him immediately. Wagner yelled in the gray's ear and slammed a pair of tiny-roweled English riding spurs into the jack's flanks. The gray snorted and bunched its muscles, then took off with a shrill squeal. Wagner's hat flew off his head, but he didn't look back.

"Here they come," Wilson shouted.

Clint grabbed the gate, swinging it shut. "Get to the station," he ordered. Wilson took off without argument, hobbling swiftly across the dusty ground on his game leg. Clint dropped the latch in place and followed him. The Cheyenne were racing through the trees, the sound of their shrill yipping shattering the early morning stillness. But they were still a hundred yards away when Clint and Wilson reached the front door.

"Give 'em hell on the way past," Clint shouted as he shouldered through the door on Wilson's heels. He elbowed the heavy door shut and dropped the oak bar into its slots. Rifle fire crashed around the big room, the din inside the stone walls deafening. Clint winced at the renewed throbbing in his head. He pushed a rifle slot open and drew his Colt. He was facing north, the broad, dusty flat, with Rocky Top a solid mass of earth and crumbling rock knifing the pale blue belly of the sky, before him. He started to push his revolver's muzzle through the slot when a spot of color near Rocky Top's base caught his eye. He pulled the Colt back, blinking. Then a slow, grim smile wormed its way across his face. "There you are," he whispered.

It was the warrior on the Appaloosa, the chief. Clint

hadn't seen him at all yesterday, and had wondered if perhaps someone else had managed to kill him. But here he was, big as life.

Clint holstered his Colt and grabbed the Whitworth. He estimated the distance at 600 yards, a far shot for such a small target, even for the heavy-barreled Whitworth, but not impossible. The light was good and there was only a hint of a breeze.

He rested the Whitworth's banded barrel on the bottom of the rifle slot and flipped the vernier sight up. He made his adjustments without rush, his fingers sliding deftly over the slim, cool columns of the sight. He tightened the eye cup last, his jaw starting to knot from the stiffness of his smile.

Bullets and flint-tipped arrows struck the stone walls of the station as a small band of warriors streaked past, but the Cheyenne were more intent on chasing Wagner than making an assault on the building. Only the warrior on the Appaloosa seemed immune to the confusion going on below him. He sat his pony proudly, staring to the southwest as if following the trail of Kane and Cantrell in his mind.

"Just hold steady," Clint breathed, thumbing a shell into the Whitworth's breech and slamming it closed. He brought the rifle to his shoulder and found his sights, lowering them slowly until the front blade completely obliterated the figure of the warrior. Clint's smile stretched. "It's about damn time," he murmured, squeezing the trigger.

CHAPTER 17

RUSTY SIGNALLED THE others to slow their horses as they guided them across the rutted path of the Santa Fe Trail. Before them a little grove of elms lay like a faded green stone set in the middle of a sun-blasted plain. Alders and reeds swayed gently in the morning breeze, running east and west from the grove of trees and marking the broad, winding course of the Arkansas River. The alders offered a likely hiding place for bushwhackers, white or red, but Rusty was more fascinated with the trail itself than with any possibility of attack.

He'd grown up in western Missouri, where tales of the Santa Fe trade—of wild, lonely stretches of emptiness linking the exotic culture of an ancient civilization, and of Indian tribes that practiced torture and cannibalism—abounded. He'd been enthralled, and more than a little cowed, by the stories he'd heard as a youngster. He'd always looked upon the men who braved such dangers as being different; not quite gods, but certainly something more than merely mortal. And now here he was, crossing that same road, following that same path.

It was, Rusty reflected as he eyed the ribbed earth, almost a disappointment. On those sections of the trail he'd viewed in eastern Kansas (where the Indians—the Otoes, Kaws, and Potowatamies—farmed rather than scalped), the road had been a narrow, graded path winding through sprawling forests and across verdant pastures. Its end had always been in sight, severed by the crest of the next hill or the next bend in the road. Danger and intrigue had always been somewhere beyond that, always just over the horizon. Rusty couldn't remember now just what he'd envisioned when he thought of the western section of the trail, but it wasn't this, this broad stretch of guttered tracks crisscrossing the Arkansas's flood plain without theme.

"Reckon we'll water the stock up ahead, take us a little breather," Kane said, glancing warily at Rusty.

Rusty just nodded. He was aware of Kane's ambivalence toward him, his cautious fear of Rusty's temper and skill with a gun, weighed against his scorn of Rusty's inexperience on the plains. A smile flickered at the corners of Rusty's mouth. Kane had once called them equals, but Rusty figured he'd drilled that notion out of the old man's head last night.

He glanced behind him at the women plodding along with their shoulders slumped, their chins dipped toward their chests. They looked worn out, exhausted, as if they'd traveled five hundred miles overnight, rather than just fifty. Ruby, as if sensing his gaze upon her, lifted her head to return his stare. Hatred glittered in her eyes, and her lips, already starting to chap from the drying wind, formed a tight, thin line. Rusty wanted to laugh at her, to cut her down a couple of notches with his callousness, but something inside stopped him. He turned away, catching at the last moment the look of contempt that crossed her face.

They rode into the trees and halted. It was a small grove, with tall, wind-cured bluestem growing under it and a litter of dead limbs, buffalo dung, and old fire pits revealing the popularity of its shelter. A weather-ratted piece of canvas was strung between a couple of the trees, the remnants of some traveler's lean-to. Rusty studied the frayed canvas contemplatively, wondering what must have happened to force someone into leaving a piece of property so far from any place where it might be replaced. A stampede? Indians? Or maybe it had just grown too burdensome to pack along anymore.

Rusty dismounted and arched his back against the knot of muscles that always formed low along his spine when he pushed too long in the saddle. He took his hat off and hung it on the saddle horn, then rolled his shirtsleeves up past his forearms. It was warm, despite the early hour, and the breeze that rippled the tall grass felt good against his clammy flesh.

Kane began untying Ruby's ankles, but Rusty noticed with amusement that he wasn't watching her closely. Although he was facing away from Rusty, he was turned enough to keep an eye on him. Grinning, Rusty stretched, then let his hands fall swiftly, slapping the leather of his holster with a loud *pop.*

Kane flinched and ducked, and Rusty laughed. "You're too jumpy, old hoss. You gotta learn to relax around friends."

"By God, you think that's funny, but it ain't," Kane flared. His jaw worked tremulously. "Don't you think I'm gonna forgit it, either. Don't you do that for a second, sonny."

Rusty nodded soberly, but the twitch at the corner of his mouth belied his expression. "Okay," he said, eyes twinkling.

"Do you think you could untie us before you shoot each other?" Ruby asked.

Kane scowled at her but didn't reply.

Rusty said, "Why sure, honey. We want you to fix us a little breakfast anyway, like proper wives. You can't do that roped to a saddle." He went to Emma's side and loosened the knots. As he coiled the rope, he looked up and smiled warmly. "Come on down, Emma. No one's gonna eat you."

The girl sniffed and her eyes welled tears, a feat Rusty found remarkable after the amount of moisture she'd shed last night. "I'm—I'm afraid, Rusty. Pro—promise you won't—won't do anything."

"Like what?" Rusty asked, grinning.

Emma blushed. *"You know."*

Laughing, Rusty replied, "Why, darlin', I'm afraid I don't know. Tell me."

"Why don't you leave her alone, Cantrell?" Ruby interrupted. "Can't you see she's scared?"

"Whew." Rusty shook his head in admiration. "You are a feisty one. I ain't so sure Kane didn't get the pick of the litter when he chose you, though he might trade if I was to ask him nice." He put his hand on his revolver. "But it's time you quit causing trouble. Understand?"

Ruby opened her mouth to speak, then closed it. She nodded silently, and Rusty grinned.

"See, you ain't so dumb."

Ruby swung a leg over the saddle and dropped to the ground, hanging onto the pommel until her legs found strength after so many hours in the saddle. Emma, younger and more agile, swung down easily. Rusty and Kane pulled the saddles off the stock and hobbled them while the women gathered wood for a fire and began preparing breakfast.

Rusty rolled a cigarette while Ruby and Emma fussed with the meal. Killing time, he made his way through the rushes to stand on the bank of the Arkansas. The river was broad and shallow here, scored by sandbars grown over with grass. A blue heron, fully four feet tall, stood on one leg at the edge of a shoal as Rusty stepped free of the rushes. It took off when it spotted him, beating the air above the river with slow, sweeping wing flaps that rippled the water until the huge bird gained altitude. Rusty watched in reverence until it glided onto a sandbar several hundred yards upstream, then raised his cigarette to his lips. After a couple of minutes Kane came up beside him, unbuttoning his fly to piss into the river.

"Been all over this country, one time or the other," Kane said above the splash of his water. "Mean, it is. As soon kill a man as let 'im pass."

"It doesn't look so mean to me," Rusty replied.

"That's 'cause you don't know it the way I do. I lived out here a good many years." He gave Rusty a gauging look. "Had me a squaw for a while."

"I figured that, old man."

"A Cheyenne, she was."

"Is that who's after us? Her father and brothers?"

"Naw. Her family was kilt last winter on the Washita. Her too, I reckon. I didn't see her among the prisoners after the battle." He sniffed and rubbed at his nose. "Was some surprised to find 'em there, I was. They'd been a traveling with old Spotted Owl's bunch afore."

Understanding dawned slowly, and Rusty looked at Kane in amazement. "You were there? On the Washita with Custer?"

Sensing his interest, Kane warmed up to the story. "Led 'em, by God. Me 'n Californy Joe and some others. Bunch of Osage scouts that hate the Cheyenne as much as I do, I reckon."

Rusty was silent a moment, trying to fathom Kane's action. "Why did you live with them, if you hated them?" he asked at last.

"Didn't hate 'em when I went to live with 'em. You gotta know redskins 'fore you kin hate 'em. That's what I found out. Crazy bastards, always wantin' this or that but never wantin' t' pay for anything. Steal you blind, they will. Even married t' one of 'em. Man gits tired of such treatment after a while, so I did some stealin' myself, when most of the bucks was off huntin' buffler. Made me quite a haul in robes and furs and such, then led Custer to the Washita. Them was glory days, sonny, or this ol' hoss wouldn't say so."

"You sound proud of it," Rusty observed in wonder.

"Well, I reckon. Kilt us a heap of Cheyenne that day, we did."

Mostly women and children and old men, from what Rusty had heard of the battle. He shook his head in disgust. "Christ, you led the soldiers to your own village?"

"Wasn't my village, I tolt you," Kane snapped. "It was ol' Black Kettle's village."

"That makes the difference, huh?"

Kane's eyes narrowed with newfound courage. "You're a mighty brave talker, Cantrell, for a goddamn outlaw. Reckon you dirtied a nest or two of your own over the years."

Rusty sighed, thinking back to Iola, and his distaste toward the old man faded some. "I reckon you're right. But at least I ain't proud of it."

"Well, I ain't as highfalutin as you are."

A horse nickered from the other side of the rushes, and Rusty swore and whirled, fighting his way through the maze of reeds and over the spongy ground that he'd dodged on the way in. He splashed water against the crotch of his canvas jeans, and almost lost his boots in the sucking black mud.

When Rusty burst through the reeds, Emma was already mounted, but Ruby was having trouble getting onto her horse without a saddle. Rusty swore and laughed in the same breath, racing across the meadow. The women had pulled the hobbles off all four horses, intending to take the extra mounts with them. If Ruby's riding skirt hadn't been so tight they might have made it, but as it was she couldn't get enough leverage to swing her leg over the animal's back. By the time she decided to just belly-flop aboard and worry about the rest later, it was too late.

Rusty was still chuckling as he grabbed Ruby's belt and yanked her off. She sprawled in front of him, cursing. Rusty stepped back, winded after his sprint from the river. Emma jerked her horse around and pounded its ribs with her heels. Rusty wanted to tell her to come on back, that she wasn't going to outrun them without a saddle, and even if she did she'd more than likely ride straight into the Cheyenne, who were bound to be on their trail by now. But before he could catch his breath, Kane's Henry roared.

Rusty swore and spun, throwing himself into the dirt and drawing his Colts. He swore again when he saw the direction of Kane's rifle, but held his fire. Looking over his shoulder, he saw Emma's horse fall, the girl's arms flailing wildly as she flipped over the animal's neck.

Ruby's mount jumped, spooking the other two horses. Rusty cursed and scrambled to his feet, but the horses, discovering they were free, wheeled and bolted back the way they'd come.

"Catch 'em, goddamnit!" Kane shrieked. "Goddamnit, catch 'em!" He came running out of the trees, as spooked as the horses but not nearly as fast.

Rusty stood silently with the Colts hanging in his hands, watching in disbelief as the horses grew small in the distance.

Clint swore even as the Whitworth rocked his shoulder. Powder smoke blossoming from the rifle's muzzle erased the distant ridge where the warrior on the Appaloosa watched Wagner's flight. But Clint didn't have to see what he could as easily feel.

He had missed.

Clint reloaded while the roiling cloud of smoke tumbled lazily out of the way. Irritation pricked at him. It had been an easy shot, and it didn't help to tell himself that even the best missed occasionally.

Rocky Top came slowly into view, its arroyo-scarred flank bare. Clint picked out the quick flash of the Appaloosa streaking westward, already well out of range. He shook his head with resignation. "I'm going to have to call you

'Cat,' " he told the shrinking figure of the Cheyenne. He'd never seen so much luck surrounding one man.

A curse erupted from the main bedroom, followed by a burst of explosive shouting. Booth came slamming through the door, his face a deep shade of red. Obscenities rolled off his tongue, peppering the air. He headed for the front door, lifting his Colt.

"Amos!" Wilson limped into the main room after him. "Amos, it's too late."

"You think I don't know that?" Booth shouted, stopping and whirling on the station manager. Spittle flew from his mouth; his face was twisted with anguish. "You think I don't know what's going on out there?"

Wilson's gaze swung helplessly to Clint. "They caught Jerome. A couple of Cheyenne must have been hiding at the eastern end of the grove. They cut him off before he could even get clear of the trees. He tried circling off the road, but . . . hell, they were on him before he could even lift a weapon."

"The bastards," Booth sobbed, his Colt dropping to his side. "The dirty bastards."

Clint shouldered past Booth and went into the bedroom. From an opened shutter he could peer out along the stage road running toward the morning sun. He spotted the mule first, lying in a heap just off the road. Then he saw Wagner's body.

The Cheyenne hadn't wasted much time on the Englishman. Clint supposed there was some satisfaction in that, however bitter. He'd seen too much Cheyenne handiwork over the years to have any illusions about what they were capable of. Sunlight glinted off Wagner's crimson pate, but other than taking his scalp and probably whatever weapons a hurried search might have yielded, they hadn't mutilated the corpse. Perhaps a fear of the Whitworth's accuracy had spurred them.

Or maybe they had other prey to chase.

Kane.

The name brought a patchwork of images to Clint's mind—panicky eyes, a narrow chin, beaded and quilled moccasins, hair white as snow and skin like old leather exposed too long to the prairie winds.

"What's your secret, old man?" Clint muttered to himself.

Wilson entered the room. "They're pulling out."

"South?"

"Yeah."

Clint's shoulders sagged. Wagner's death had been in vain. But had it? he asked himself, remembering the Englishman's quiet courage, his desire to die like a warrior. And his death had proven to Clint that it was Kane the Cheyenne had been after all along.

Dropping to the floor, he said, "We'll have to follow as best we can, and hope for a chance to get around them."

"Let's go," Wilson said grimly.

CHAPTER 18

NOON CAME AND went, and still they trudged onward, walking west now, with the Arkansas River to their right, hidden behind a fringe of low, barren hills.

Kane led, pushing forward in a tireless, rolling gait. His head swiveled constantly as he scanned the serrated horizon. He carried a bull's-eye canteen of Union vintage from one skinny, sloping shoulder, and an extra cartridge belt for his Henry on the other.

The women followed, stumbling now and again as heat and fatigue sapped their strength. They both carried saddlebags filled with food, and Ruby carried a second canteen, emptied an hour before.

Rusty brought up the rear with a canvas waterbag sloshing wetly against his hip. The waterbag held less than half a gallon, and Kane's canteen was almost empty. It wasn't much, but Rusty figured it would last them until dark if they were careful.

He had almost killed Kane that morning, watching the horses disappear over the distant rim of the horizon. He knew they weren't likely to stop for miles, and even then they would be spooky and hard to catch. Pushed, they might run all the way back to Cottonwood Station. Slowly, he'd turned toward the old frontiersman, standing with his back to him, the Henry sagging in his hands. It would have been easy to put a bullet between Kane's bony shoulder blades then. So damned easy.

But he needed Kane, now more than ever. He needed his skills and his sense of direction, and most important, he needed the map that was etched inside the old man's head. Without him, Rusty would be forced to follow the meandering path of the Santa Fe Trail as it skirted the Arkansas, forced to rely on guesswork and luck. Those were bad cards in any man's hand, Rusty figured, and with the Cheyenne bound to follow, he wasn't willing to risk the odds.

So he'd holstered his Colts and kept his mouth shut while the old fool ranted at the women, blaming them for his own stupidity. Rusty had stepped in only when Kane started to slap them around, telling him they still needed the women, needed someone to tote the saddlebags and the water.

So they stumbled on under a blazing sun while the wind picked up and buffeted their bodies and the sandy soil pulled at their hot, aching feet until the muscles in the calves of their legs screamed for rest. Stumbled on with the fear in the backs of their minds and a growing hatred for each other, and all with the knowledge that the Cheyenne were coming—as sure as the sun and sand, they were coming.

Clint kept the dun at a hard lope and let the miles tick off behind him. Sweat darkened the horse's flanks, and a thick, ropy lather had built up around the cinch. The big, rangy gelding held the grueling pace without complaint, but the strain was starting to show. The dun's breath was labored, its gait rough.

Wilson, riding Clyde Cooper's big roan, had no trouble keeping up. The roan was equal to the dun, and probably superior in endurance.

They had left Grady on Clint's packhorse behind the first ridge south of the station. It had been Wilson's idea, but Clint quickly saw the wisdom in his thinking.

"Grady, I want you to circle around the station and ride like hell for Fort Larned." Wilson paused, as if awaiting the young shotgun's protest. It wasn't long in coming.

"Uh-uh. I'm coming with you."

Patiently, Wilson said, "You won't be able to keep up, son, and we can't wait for you. Besides, someone needs to get word to the army. Greg Potts never came in, and Lord knows what happened to him. And there's no guarantee Clint or I will make it back. Someone has to get word to Larned, get some soldiers down here."

Grady swallowed visibly, face working. "Damnit, Mr. Wilson . . ."

"I know, son. I can see how much you love Emma, and I can understand how you might want to go after her. But the best way to help her now is for you to go to Larned."

Grady shook his head reluctantly. "Okay, I'll go."

They left Grady at the bottom of the ridge and pushed on while the sun broke free of the eastern horizon and began its slow climb toward noon. The Cheyenne were still somewhere ahead of them, their trail easy to follow across the dry, sandy hills, the tracks less than a half hour old.

Their numbers puzzled Clint, and for a long time he kept looking over his shoulder, half expecting a trap. But no Indians appeared behind them, and in time he came to accept the fact that he and Wilson were following less than a dozen warriors.

Wilson had noticed the smaller number of tracks as well. Pulling their mounts to a walk around midmorning, he ranged alongside Clint. "What happened to the others?" he asked.

Clint shrugged. "Hard to say. Maybe they gave up. Or maybe they're still back at the station."

Wilson's face took on a worried cast, but he didn't voice any doubts. Clint figured it was enough that the odds had been cut as much as they had. Nine or ten Cheyenne weren't going to be any picnic, but it beat the thirty or so warriors that had pounded the station for the past couple of days.

They picked up the pace again, not attempting to over-

take the Cheyenne or circle around them just yet, but
content to let them set the pace for a while. As the sun
began its downward slide the land began to change, becoming more broken and barren. They were approaching
the sandhills, with the Arkansas just beyond.

Clouds drifted across the blue bowl of sky, blanketing
the land with their shadows. The wind was hot in the
sunshine, but almost refreshing in the sprawling pockets
of shade. There was a hint of rain in the air, the slight
electrical charge of a storm advancing from somewhere
beyond the western rim of prairie.

It was midafternoon when they passed through a notch
in the hills and spotted the river, perhaps a mile ahead.
Pulling their mounts to a halt, Clint pointed to the southwest with his chin. In the far distance, the Cheyenne were
just entering the hills south of the river. They were riding
at a hard gallop, as if the trail they followed had freshened.

Medicine Wolf's pulse quickened as he led the others into
the hills. Wet Otter rode at his side, but the young warrior's
keen eyesight and superb tracking skills weren't needed
anymore. The white-eyes had lost their ponies, and now
they were afoot, making a desperate flight for the next
station.

Medicine Wolf wanted to laugh at the futility of their
efforts. Lost His Horse and a dozen others had burned
that station to the ground four days before, killing everyone inside. Even if White Hawk did manage to reach the
station, he would find only ashes and bloated, mutilated
corpses to hide behind.

But Medicine Wolf knew the traitor would not make it
that far. In attempting a shortcut, White Hawk had led
the white-eyes into a tangle of low, steep-sided hills, their
flanks covered with sand that would quickly sap their
strength. The People would catch up somewhere inside
that bleak, broken country. They would quickly overpower

the weakened whites, and then they would have their revenge. Against the man with the two pistols and the women first. White Hawk they would save to take with them, back to their village along the Washita.

They pushed their wearied ponies, eager now to complete what had taken them nearly nine moons to reach. The trail grew fresher by the mile, the two-pistoled man's tracks weaving now, the women stumbling often, occasionally falling. Only the prints of White Hawk's moccasins remained straight and unwavering, and Medicine Wolf was impressed by the old man's strength and determination. It would be wise to remember not only his strength, Medicine Wolf mused, but also his cunning. Perhaps the traitor should have been named after the fox, or coyote.

Topping a low rise, Medicine Wolf jerked his Appaloosa to a sudden halt. The others crowded up around him, yipping and shouting as the view below them became clear.

The whites had reached the middle of a broad basin, and were resting at the edge of a buffalo wallow. Except for the wallow, there was no shelter within five hundred yards in any direction.

Lost His Horse pushed his pony forward, crowing loudly. "It is as Medicine Wolf said. We have found White Hawk."

Lucky In Love snorted derisively. "We have caught *up* with White Hawk. My brother forgets that we have not yet caught him."

"It is the same," Looks Far answered bluntly. "White Hawk is ours. I have seen this basin before, in a vision brought to me by Sparrow." He looked at Medicine Wolf, his expression sad. "It will be as that vision, old friend."

Medicine Wolf nodded somberly, remembering the whole of Looks Far's prophecy—his brothers had dragged White Hawk away on the end of a rope, south toward the Washita, but Medicine Wolf had not been among them.

He took a deep breath, drawing the sun-washed fragrance of the short, brown grass into his lungs. To the west the clouds were piling high and craggy, like snowy cliffs with flat, black bellies. Medicine Wolf nodded. It was good to see the storm approaching, to know that tonight the wind would blow with the vengeance of squaws turned loose on a prisoner, and that lightning would stroke the plains, torching the dried grass with the cleansing breath of fire. It was good also to see the sky above him like a pale blue mantel, and the muted shades of red and blue that tinged the hills. He felt the sweat of the Appaloosa on his thighs, and the slightly greasy touch of the single rawhide rein in his hands. He heard the rustle of the wind in the grass, and the stomp of hooves. It was good that he was aware of these things, and that Man Above had granted him the gift of that awareness. He missed only Red Willow Woman and his son, who waited on the Other Side.

"It is a good day to die," he told Looks Far.

"*Aiee*," Looks Far shrilled under his breath, so that only Medicine Wolf heard. "I will sing for my brother, Medicine Wolf."

Smiling, Medicine Wolf lifted the Appaloosa's rein and rode down off the low rise at a lope.

Kane's face paled to a sickly white. He stood, the bull's-eye canteen falling from his lap, spilling precious water into the cracked hardpan of the wallow.

"Hey," Rusty said in alarm, leaning toward the canteen. But before he could grab it he caught a flash of movement from the corner of his eye and froze.

Emma screamed.

A chill ran down Rusty's spine, and his scalp crawled. "My God," Rusty breathed.

Whimpering, Emma fell to her knees. "No," she moaned. "Oh, please, no."

Ruby was the first to recover. She stood, facing the party

of Indians streaming down the low rise. "This is it," she said grimly. "Cantrell, give me one of your pistols."

Rusty would have as soon given up his legs as one of his Colts, but he carried a short-barreled pocket revolver in a waist holster snugged against the small of his back. He palmed it and handed it to Ruby. "It's only a five-shooter, and I keep the chamber under the hammer empty. You've got four shots. Make 'em count."

Ruby grabbed Emma and pulled her below the rim of the wallow. Rusty flopped down beside them.

Kane crouched on the far side of the wallow, eyes darting wildly. Licking at cracked lips, he said, "We can trade the women, Cantrell. Cheyenne like white women. Set a heap of store by 'em, by God."

"Bullshit." Rusty winked at Ruby, feeling a sudden rush of warmth toward this iron-willed woman beside him.

"They will, I tell you. Let me talk to 'em."

"Not yet," Rusty replied. "Get up here with that rifle, Kane."

Kane crawled across the wallow on his hands and knees and bellied down where he could peer over the grass-furred lip. The Cheyenne were still nearly four hundred yards away, too far yet for any weapon they had with them. Remembering Dawson's long range Whitworth, Rusty muttered a curse.

"Eleven," Ruby announced tightly. "I count only eleven."

Rusty watched the advancing line of warriors coming down off the rise. "Hell, eleven ain't such bad odds," he said, brightening. "I faced worse than that in the war, and ate a good breakfast afterward."

"These ain't soldier boys," Kane countered darkly.

"A fight is a fight," Rusty replied cheerfully, cocking his Colts and squirming against the side of the wallow to make himself more comfortable. The Cheyenne were about three hundred yards away now, coming straight at them. Their shrill yips and howls reminded Rusty of the hoarse rebel yells he and his companions often used during the war to intimidate their enemy. Rusty laughed, a quick, rattling burst of nervous energy, and raised his own head to shout back at the approaching Cheyenne.

Kane levered a round into the chamber, lifted the Henry's rear ladder sight, and thumbed the veed notch about halfway up.

"This is your chance, Kane," Rusty said without cynicism. "You can pick 'em off like flies with that rifle."

"It ain't gonna be that easy," Kane growled, pressing his cheek to the Henry's smooth walnut stock and sighting down the slim octagon barrel. He squinted, steadying the rifle against the wallow's shaggy lip, squeezing off his first round when the Indians were still some two hundred yards away.

The Henry's report was a sharp, ear-popping crack, echoless in the middle of the flat basin. Rusty frowned but didn't speak. Kane's shot kicked up a geyser of dust about twenty yards in front of the nearest warriors.

"A Henry ain't like my old Hawkens rifle," Kane explained in a quavering voice, as if needing to talk now, to hear the sound of someone's voice, even his own, to calm his nerves. He jacked another round into the chamber, the spent cartridge flipping over his shoulder. "It ain't got the range, carrying only forty grains of powder. It's more of a close-up weapon, something between a pistol and a good heavy-bore rifle."

The Henry cracked again, the bullet whining high.

"Damnit, man, settle down," Rusty said tautly.

Kane's breath quickened. He rubbed at his eyes, then chambered a third round. The Cheyenne were within a hundred and fifty yards now. The pounding of their ponies' hooves could be felt through the ground like a low-keyed humming. The sound of their shrill yells raked at Rusty's nerves.

Kane fired a third time, and a Cheyenne on a blaze-faced bay tumbled from the back of his mount.

The Cheyenne split abruptly, skirting wide around the saucer-shaped depression gouged into the basin. Rusty scrambled to cover the west side of the wallow, but held his fire. The Indians loosened a few arrows and a couple of shots from their muzzle-loading trade rifles as they passed, but at seventy-five yards and from the back of running mounts, their aim was as wild as Kane's. Only one rifle ball came close, plowing a furrow through the grass in front of the wallow. Kane kept up a steady firing, but he was rattled now, and his shots all went wide.

The two groups of warriors curved back in on each other about two hundred yards out, passing and swinging back toward the wallow.

"Bastards!" Kane shrieked. "Sonsabitches!" He scuttled across the wallow, firing as he went.

"Hold your fire," Rusty bellowed. "They're too far away yet."

Kane slowed, then stopped, looking over his shoulder at Rusty. Terror pulled at the muscles in his face, filling his eyes with dread. Spittle traced his jaw. "They're gonna overrun us, sure as hell. We gotta give 'em the woman, Cantrell! It's our only chance."

Rusty lifted a revolver. "Not yet."

"It's our only chance, I tell you!" Kane screamed.

Rusty snapped a shot into the bank beside Kane's elbow, but the old frontiersman never flinched. Fear gripped him with iron claws, smothering reason.

Shoot him! a voice in Rusty's mind shouted. *Shoot him before he shoots you!*

"Just settle down, Kane," Rusty said, ignoring the voice. He nodded toward the prairie. "They're within range."

Kane turned back, cursing as he shouldered the Henry. He began firing, pumping lead in the general direction of the Cheyenne, but jerking the trigger with each shot. Not an Indian fell as Kane emptied his rifle. Falling back from the edge of the wallow, he began to reload, fumbling the cartridges from the shellbelt at his waist.

Rusty slid forward, waiting until the Indians were within sixty yards before opening fire with his Colts. He took his time, firing methodically, and his shots began to tell. He knocked a warrior askew on his pony and wounded another in the thigh. In the face of his revolvers, the Cheyenne quickly split, streaking past the wallow on either side, but closing in to less than forty yards this time, well within range for their bows and rifles. Arrows sliced the air above the wallow, and bullets gouged holes in the dirt around them. Miraculously, no one was injured.

The Indians didn't pause. At one hundred yards they suddenly wheeled their ponies and charged down on them again, and Rusty's stomach turned liquid. This was it, he told himself, lifting his nearly emptied revolvers. This time they wouldn't veer away.

CHAPTER 19

MEDICINE WOLF BENT low along the Appaloosa's neck. A scream of victory, like the scream of an eagle closing its claws around a rabbit, welled in his throat. The Appaloosa's hooves flashed above the backward flow of the prairie, the pony's muscles rippling smoothly. A war club carved from a piece of Osage orange dangled from his wrist by a leather thong. He shoved his rifle into a leather loop fastened to the saddle and swung the club into his hand.

He could see White Hawk clearly. The traitor was on his knees in the middle of the wallow, frantically sliding brass shells down the tube of his repeating rifle. The other man was also reloading. Only the woman who had escaped from the coach held a weapon as if ready to fire, but Medicine Wolf could see the terror on her face from a hundred yards away. He knew, with the certainty of an eagle's wisdom and a wolf's cunning, that he would not die by the hands of this woman.

Perhaps Looks Far's vision had been blurred, Medicine Wolf thought. Perhaps he would not die today after all.

Lucky In Love rode beside him, bellowing like an enraged, wounded buffalo. He carried a tack-studded Leman rifle in his right hand, but he hadn't fired it yet. He had saved his single shot until he was close enough to make it count.

Lucky In Love never got to touch off his shot. He slammed forward along his pony's neck, the Leman spinning from his hand. Blood sprouted from a gaping hole in his back, turning into a red mist that brushed Medicine

Wolf's thigh. Lucky In Love slid from his pony, and the Appaloosa dodged the fallen body.

"Soldiers!" Lost His Horse shouted, jerking his mount to a plunging stop. Medicine Wolf hauled back on the Appaloosa's rein, pulling the stocky pony around. But there were no longknives behind them, only a tattered gray-white cloud of powder smoke on a distant rise.

Clint thumbed a fresh shell in the Whitworth's breech and slapped it shut with an upward movement of his palm. As the powder smoke cleared he saw the Indians milling below him, their charge abruptly demoralized by the Whitworth's unerring accuracy.

As Clint cocked the Whitworth, Wilson broke out of the hills to the east and raced the long-limbed roan across the basin. The Cheyenne spotted him immediately, and several quirted their poines toward him to cut him off before he reached the shallow buffalo wallow.

Wilson was forced to rein away from the wallow, running the roan south across the basin. A couple of Cheyenne followed him, but Clint doubted they would ever catch up. The road was too fast, and it had staying power to match any mustang.

Clint brought his attention back to the larger group below him, lowering the Whitworth's sights until they framed the warrior on the Appaloosa. Taking a deep breath, Clint squeezed the trigger.

Medicine Wolf's heart sank. The other warriors spread out, unconsciously creating a broad, empty field around the dancing, wall-eyed Appaloosa. A cloud of powder smoke blossomed from the top of the ridge as they watched. Medicine Wolf's blood went cold as the smoke formed a familiar image, the shape of a white wolf—his spirit helper—turning away.

A bullet slammed into Medicine Wolf's chest, knocking

him from his saddle. The ground struck his back and shoulders, driving his breath away. He tried to draw another, but the air wouldn't come. His lungs had quit working. He saw Looks Far come into view above him, still mounted, and knew by the look of shock on his friend's face that he had also seen the wolf turn away.

Alone, Medicine Wolf began his final journey.

Rusty stared in disbelief at the milling Indians. His capper, still attached to one of the Colt's nipples, slipped from his fingers. Coming up beside him on his knees, Kane murmured unintelligibly.

"Clint!" Ruby sobbed. Her shoulders sagged at last, and she tipped her head forward to hide the tears streaming down her cheeks.

Rusty lifted his gaze to the low rise, nearly five hundred yards away. Near its crest a tiny puff of powder smoke was whisked from sight. He could just make out the figure of a man sitting with his knees up, a long, heavy-looking rifle shelved away from him, as if resting on cross-sticks. It was Dawson, all right.

"Hell, I'm almost happy to see the bastard myself," Rusty said aloud.

A flashy, riderless red and white Appaloosa pranced away from the churning, gesturing knot of warriors, trailing a twenty-foot jawline rein. As the horse approached the wallow, it veered suddenly away, but Kane lunged after it on hands and knees, snagging the rein and scooting back into the wallow before the Cheyenne spotted him. He quickly reeled the horse after him.

"Jesus," Kane was chanting in an almost prayerlike whisper as he pulled the Appaloosa closer. "Jesus, Jesus." His gaze darted between the horse and the milling warriors, but his rifle was trained loosely on Rusty and the women.

"Where you going, Kane?" Rusty asked easily, standing.

"Just never you mind, sonny. I'm through with outlaws, and I'm cutting this partnership short."

Rusty pulled the pencil-thin capper away from the Colt and let it drop. "Running out?"

Kane turned to face him, his finger on the Henry's trigger. "By God, I'm tired of takin' orders from the likes of you, Cantrell. You pull your horns in, or I'll shoot them off."

"If you're fast enough," Rusty said evenly.

Kane's eyes widened, and he stopped pulling the Appaloosa in. He licked his lips in a gauging manner.

"I'll be taking that horse," Rusty said evenly, planting his feet wide and sliding his thumb over the Colt's hammer. He smiled, reading the fear in Kane's eyes. Even with the Henry aimed at Rusty's chest, Kane was still intimidated.

"Reckon not," Kane said finally.

"Reckon so, old man."

"Damnit, boy, it's me they want. Don't you see that?"

"Stay here and trade 'em the women," Rusty said mockingly.

"You bastard," Kane cried. "You dirty—"

Kane's sentence was smothered by the hammering blast of the Henry. Rusty's eyes widened as the .44 slug took him low in the chest, slamming him backward. He grunted sharply, and the Colt seemed to leap from his hand, bouncing across the short buffalo grass. He fell on his back with his arms splayed, darkness rimming his vision, funneling it toward the sky. Pink, bubbling froth trickled from the corner of his mouth. "I'll be damned," he rasped, the words audible to his ears alone. "The old bastard was more afraid of the Cheyenne than he was of me."

Clint studied the wallow. The distance was too great to make out any detail, but he recognized the Appaloosa easily enough, and Kane's white hair. Kane was swinging atop the horse, jerking it around and racing away from the wallow.

Those Indians who were left quickly followed, but it was the warriors who'd chased Wilson that sealed Kane's fate. As soon as Kane left the wallow, they abandoned their chase and wheeled their ponies to cut the old frontiersman off. Kane, looking over his shoulder at those pursuing him, ran right into the others.

Clint's mouth went dry as a warrior on a buckskin slammed his mount into Kane's Appaloosa. Both horses went down in a cloud of dust. The sound of the collision, of shouting men and squealing ponies, carried faintly on the wind. The other Indians quickly swarmed into the turmoil of pitching mounts and swirling dust.

Slowly, the confusion settled, the dust cleared. Clint cocked the Whitworth expectantly. Wilson had wheeled his roan around as soon as the Cheyenne gave up on him, and quickly circled back to the wallow. He was there now, the roan ground-tied a few yards away. The body of Indians broke apart, and three of them rode back toward the wallow at a walk, leading the Appaloosa and a second mount. They swung wide around the wallow and paused only long enough to load the bodies of their dead comrades on the riderless horses. Then two of the Cheyenne rode away, leading the pack animals with their grisly loads. But the third hesitated, standing in front of his mount and facing the rise where Clint waited with the Whitworth.

Then, using his hands in the common sign language of the plains tribes, the Indian began to speak: *I am Looks Far Man,* the Indian said. *We have taken the traitor, White Hawk, as Man Above instructed. Now we will go, unless you wish to fight some more.*

Clint let his breath out in a long sigh. Laying the Whitworth aside, he stood, glad now that he had learned to speak with his hands while trading with old Bill Hanks.

Gesturing broadly, because of the distance, he replied: *We have fought enough, you and I. It is time for peace.*

The Cheyenne swung onto his pony and rode back to the others at a walk. When he reached them, the Indians whirled and set out at a rapid pace across the basin, riding south toward the Indian Nations.

They pulled Kane behind them on the end of a long rope, his screams of terror fading as the wind picked up.

It was over, finished with a suddenness that left them all chilled and slightly bewildered.

Clint pocketed his spent cartridges and retrieved the dun. Ruby came out to meet him. Behind her, Wilson stood in the middle of the wallow with his Spencer in hand, his free arm curved protectively around Emma's shoulders while she cried into his chest. Clint could just make out Cantrell's body, spread-eagled at the edge of the wallow.

Ruby stopped and tried a smile that eased some of the tension from her face. "Hello, Clint."

He slid from his saddle and took her in his arms. "Are you okay?" he asked gently.

She put her arms around him and nodded. "Yeah, I am now."

She tipped her head back, her green eyes drilling into his gray ones. "A couple of pieces of driftwood floating across the prairie," she said, smiling. "How long can that last?"

It took him a moment to catch up. Then he smiled, and said, "I guess we'll just have to see."

If you have enjoyed this book and would like to receive details about other Walker Western titles, please write to:

Western Editor
Walker and Company
720 Fifth Avenue
New York, NY 10019

VERMILLION
PUBLIC LIBRARY
VERMILLION, S.D.

DISCARDED
BY
VERMILLION PUBLIC
LIBRARY